STABLE RIVALS

Carole took a step back. She swallowed hard. "I . . ." She stopped. She couldn't think of a single thing to say. She was in utter shock over what had just happened. *She* had been given a lecture about riding. And by a girl who had arrived at Pine Hollow *five minutes ago*. Who the heck did Andrea Barry think she was?

"Listen . . . ," Carole began again. She still didn't know how to put it into words. How could she tell Andrea that she was the best junior rider at Pine Hollow? That Andrea ought to be listening to her—and would be, very, very soon?

THE SADDLE CLUB

SILVER STIRRUPS

BONNIE BRYANT

A SKYLARK BOOK

NEW YORK • TORONTO • LONDON • SYDNEY • AUCKLAND

RL 5, 009–012

SILVER STIRRUPS

A Bantam Skylark Book / April 1997

ISBN 0-553-48420-6

Published simultaneously in the United States and Canada.

PRINTED IN THE UNITED STATES OF AMERICA

OPM   0 9 8 7 6 5 4 3 2 1

*I would like to express my special thanks
to Caitlin Macy for her help
in the writing of this book.*

CAROLE HANSON WATCHED intently as the horse and rider flew over the course of jumps. The pair took a brush fence at the end of the ring and turned toward home. "Easy, Prancer, don't rush now. Come on, Lisa, keep her collected," Carole murmured.

It was almost as if Lisa Atwood could hear Carole's advice. She sat back in the saddle and steadied the bay mare for the final fence, a three-foot vertical. Prancer swiveled her ears back and forth, slowed almost imperceptibly, and met the jump in stride. When she landed on the opposite side, Carole could hear Lisa's joyful exclamation. "Good girl, Prancer! Good girl!"

Carole grinned as Lisa came trotting up to the group of horses and riders. "Nice going, Lisa!" she called.

It always made Carole happy to see her friends ride well, especially her *best* friends, Lisa and Stevie—short for Stephanie—Lake. The three girls took riding lessons at Pine Hollow Stables from the owner of the stables, Max Regnery. Max was notoriously stingy with compliments. But except for a couple of minor errors—coming too close to the brush, letting her reins get sloppy in the air—Lisa had put in an excellent ride. Even Max would have to acknowledge it, Carole thought.

"All right, everyone, comments for Lisa's ride?" Max demanded, walking over to the side of the ring to address the group. Max often asked his students to critique one another's performances as part of their lesson.

"I thought it was perfect!" Betsy Cavanaugh gushed.

A couple of students echoed her comment.

Max looked impatient as he nodded. "Yes, yes. . . . Anyone else?"

Stevie spoke up. "I think it's finally dawned on Prancer that it's not the fastest horse that wins!"

The group laughed. Prancer was a Thoroughbred that had started out as a racehorse on the track. It had taken her a while to adjust to being a lesson horse for Max and a Pony Club mount for Lisa. Sometimes she rushed but got lazy at the same time. Then she jumped flat and ran the risk of knocking poles down with her feet.

"Anybody have some constructive criticism?" Max inquired. "A word of advice that might help Lisa and Prancer in the schooling show?"

"The schooling show!" Stevie exclaimed, clapping a hand to her mouth. "I completely forgot!"

Carole grinned. Only Stevie could get so preoccupied with her scheming and pranks that she would forget about the Annual Spring Schooling Show at Pine Hollow.

"Why doesn't that surprise me, Stephanie?" Max asked dryly. Having taught most of the girls for several years, Max was well aware of their personality quirks.

Max's schooling shows were a Pine Hollow tradition. A schooling show was a low-key competition, hosted by the stable and open to anyone who boarded a horse at Pine Hollow or took lessons there. Some locals and friends were also invited, and Max would usually ask a colleague of his in the horse business to do the judging. It was a great way for the riders to practice competing without the pressure and expense of going to a real show.

Carole could feel Max looking at her. As the most experienced of the junior riders, Max counted on her to catch mistakes that the others might miss. She took a hand off the reins of her horse, Starlight, and held it up.

"Yes, Carole? Do you have some suggestions for how Lisa could improve her ride?"

"Just one or two little things. If she had steadied Prancer before the brush jump instead of after, Prancer wouldn't have had to pop it. Also, since the horses always get strong once they're headed toward the barn, checking her earlier might have counteracted that," Carole suggested. She glanced at Lisa and saw that her friend was nodding seriously.

Max was nodding, too, his eyes approving. "And how could Lisa keep Prancer from rushing, Carole?"

"She could keep her reins more organized over the fences instead of throwing her hands forward," Carole replied promptly.

Max nodded again. "Those were the two comments I was hoping to hear." Carole felt a rush of pride. "Do you understand, Lisa?" Max went on. "You've got to ride her *over* the fences as well as before and after them, all right? And Carole's right about the barn: We all know by now that every horse in the world is going to speed up when he's 'going home.' Got it?"

"Got it," Lisa said with confidence. "It all makes sense."

"Good. All in all, though, Lisa, a good course," said Max gruffly.

Lisa beamed, and Carole and Stevie grinned at her. "Thanks, Max," Lisa said lightly. "And thank *you*, Carole!" she whispered, as Carole tightened up her reins in preparation for her ride.

"Wait a second, Carole," Max said. He waved to Red O'Malley, the head stable hand, who was waiting down at the end of the ring. When Max caught Red's attention, he called, "Raise them six inches!"

Carole smiled as she walked and trotted Starlight to wake him up before jumping. It was just like Max to raise the fences for her, to give her a more challenging course. It was also just like him to rely on her to provide the comments he was waiting for. Carole was aware of her status as the best junior rider at Pine Hollow. She had the highest Pony Club rating of Max's students, as well as the best show record.

Luckily, Carole thought, she didn't have the kind of friends who were jealous. Stevie and Lisa understood that Carole's success as a rider was a result of many things: talent, hard work, and an unwavering dedication to horses.

All three girls were horse-crazy. That was one of the

main requirements for joining The Saddle Club, the group they had started. But Carole was the horse-craziest of the three of them. She lived and breathed horses, 100 percent of the time. She might forget school tests, doctor's appointments, or plans she had made with her father, Colonel Hanson; but she would never, ever forget about the upcoming schooling show, not for a second.

"Okay, Carole, whenever you're ready!" Max called.

Carole tightened up her reins and cantered toward the first jump, a white picket fence. Starlight's ears were pricked: Jumping was what he loved best! To Carole's delight, he soared over the picket, then the two oxers, the coop, the ditch, the in-and-out, the brush, and, finally, the vertical rail. The lesson group broke into spontaneous applause when she rejoined them.

"Starlight looked great!" said Polly Giacomin. "I love the way he snaps his knees up over the fences."

Carole smiled. She had trained Starlight, so any compliment to her horse was like a compliment to her.

"Okay, who wants to start?" Max asked.

Carole was just the tiniest bit surprised. She'd thought that there was a chance—granted, a very small chance—that Max wouldn't criticize her course at all. Starlight had jumped like a pro.

"But Max, Starlight looked like he was ready to go to the American Horse Show!" Stevie protested.

Max nodded, a hint of a smile on his lips. "Ye-es . . . I agree. Starlight has an excellent, natural jumping form."

Carole frowned slightly. "Natural jumping form" didn't say much about her training abilities. And why was Max smiling?

Betsy Cavanaugh stuck a hand up. "I thought Carole kept him at a good, steady pace throughout the course," she volunteered. A couple of others murmured concurrence.

Now Max looked truly amused. "That's a good point, Betsy." He glanced around. "So nobody has any criticism whatsoever for *Carole?*"

Carole was starting to feel defensive. Did Max have to *beg* them to criticize her? Normally Veronica diAngelo would have jumped in with a lot of problems that she'd made up—out of sheer jealousy. But with the rich, snobbish girl away on one of her many vacations, Carole had been anticipating more praise than criticism.

Then, out of the corner of her eyes, Carole saw

Lisa's hand go up tentatively. She turned to listen. Even though Lisa hadn't been riding nearly as long as Carole had, she was a good observer.

"Yes, Lisa?"

"Do you mean criticism for Carole apart from Starlight?" she inquired.

"Yes, Lisa, that's exactly what I mean."

"Well, this is really picky, but I noticed her reins getting a little long," Lisa said. "Just like mine," she added hastily.

"Is that all?" Max asked.

Lisa nodded.

"All right," said Max. "Look, guys. You and I know that Carole is a very experienced rider and that Starlight's specialty is jumping." Carole was about to relax happily when Max continued. "But that knowledge shouldn't prevent you from being sharp judges." He turned and spoke to Carole. "If you think about it, Carole, I think you'll admit that you let your own position slip a lot during that ride. You sat back and let Starlight go on autopilot. That worked today. But what about tomorrow? And next week? It won't take him long to realize if you're slouching on the job. It's something that haunts all successful horse-rider combinations: being too easy on yourself. Remember, and this goes for everyone, always challenge yourself and your horse. Unless," Max added wryly, "you decide you'd be happy moseying down a trail for the next ten years.

"All right, everyone, lesson's over! Cool out your horses and meet in the tack room as soon as you're done! I've got an announcement to make!"

A HALF HOUR LATER, the same group reassembled in the stables' tack room.

Lisa and Carole sat side by side on a sawhorse next to a row of saddles. "You okay, Carole?" Lisa whispered.

Carole nodded and managed to smile. Lisa must have seen how taken aback she'd been by Max's criticism. She knew he was right, but it was hard to hear, all the same. "Yeah, I'll survive," Carole muttered.

Up in the front of the room, Stevie, as usual, was clowning around, imitating previous judges they'd had for the schooling show.

Max entered and caught her in the act. "What's that, your Mrs. Hayes impression?" he asked, not missing a beat.

Stevie grimaced and took a seat.

"That's one comedy act you'd better retire, Stevie," Max advised.

"Why, is she judging again?" Stevie asked.

"She's not judging the schooling show, if that's what you mean," said Max. "But she is judging Briarwood."

"Briarwood?" Stevie repeated, failing to understand. Briarwood, as all the girls knew, was short for the Briarwood Horse Show, a top-level, A-rated horse show in which The Saddle Club had once competed. "But why should we care who's judging Bri—?" Stevie stopped midsentence, her eyes wide.

During the pause the door to the tack room swung open and Red O'Malley joined them.

"Red, Stevie wants to know why she should care who's judging Briarwood," Max said, his eyes twinkling.

"Well, Stevie," Red said playfully, "I guess you should always care who's judging a horse show you're riding in."

A loud squeal of joy rose up from the group. "We got invited to ride at Briarwood again?" Carole cried, all thoughts of Max's criticism forgotten.

Briarwood was such an important show that its junior riders competed by invitation only. The previous year the show committee had invited Max to bring a handful of his best students. But Max hadn't been able to promise his riders that they would be invited again.

10

Now he grinned. "I just heard from the show committee about numbers. Everyone in this room is invited to go. We've got two weeks plus the schooling show to practice."

Everyone started talking at once, shouting out questions to Red and Max.

"Quiet down for two seconds!" Max cried, laughing good-naturedly. "Let me finish giving you the basic information. Let's see . . . Oh, yes, I'll post this class list on the bulletin board outside my office so that each of you can decide what to enter. There are a number of different classes—even more than last year. And the big news is—"

"Bigger than Briarwood?" Stevie interrupted. "But Briarwood's the biggest news around!"

"No, not *bigger* than Briarwood," Max said patiently. "This has to do with Briarwood." He looked down to consult the class schedule, then read aloud: " 'This year, for the first time, the sponsorship committee of the Briarwood Horse Show is proud to offer the Silver Stirrups Trophy to be awarded to the junior rider who, in the opinion of the judges, best exemplifies the spirit of horsemastership—' "

"Speak English!" Stevie wailed.

"It's a trophy for the best all-around junior rider,"

Carole said quickly. She'd read enough programs and won enough championships to be able to translate horse show program gibberish.

"But Carole, you have enough silver to polish already!" Stevie groaned.

Everyone laughed. They all knew that Carole's bedroom was decorated with the cups, plates, and ribbons she'd started winning almost as soon as she started riding.

Max smiled warmly at Carole. "It would be great to see the Briarwood trophy come to Pine Hollow. But," he said sternly, "remember what I said: The purpose of any competition is to challenge oneself and one's horse!"

Still, Carole felt a shiver go down her spine. She sensed the other riders glancing at her. It almost felt as if she'd won the trophy already . . .

As she savored the moment, oblivious to the excited din that rose up when Max finished, there was a loud rumbling in the driveway. Carole recognized the sound of a horse van pulling in.

"That'll be the new horse," Max said to Red. "Will you go make sure his stall is ready?"

"Righto, boss," Red said, and headed out.

"Oh, and Carole? Would you do me a favor and go see about unloading the horse?" Carole snapped back to attention. "His owner was very anxious that he be handled with extreme care."

"Valuable?" Carole guessed.

"You bet. Fancy junior hunter from New England; a big winner up there, I think. I've got to go to my desk and make sure his papers are in order, and then I'll be right out," said Max.

Pleased that he had chosen her for the job, Carole followed Max out the door. It was clear that he trusted her to deal with important matters at the stables. And, seeing the look he'd given her, Carole knew that Max believed she was Pine Hollow's best chance for the Silver Stirrups Trophy at Briarwood.

It wasn't until she got to the driveway that Carole fully absorbed what Max had been saying about the horse that was arriving in the van. She pursed her lips for a second. "Fancy *junior* hunter?" she repeated.

As THE HUGE horse van rumbled to a stop, Carole ran to greet the driver.

"Is this Pine Hollow Stables?" the man inquired.

"Sure is," Carole replied. "Can I help you unload him?"

"That would be great!" the man said. "I'll let the ramp down and then you can lead him off."

"Did he give you any trouble?" Carole asked as the driver stepped down from the cab of the van.

The man shook his head. "This one? Nah. He knows the drill. He's been shipped all over the East Coast for shows. His rider competes almost every weekend."

For some reason, that wasn't the answer Carole had been hoping to receive. She made herself smile, though. "That's good news. It's always great to get new talent here."

"Oh, you're getting talent, all right. Just wait'll you get a look at this boy," said the driver in an appreciative tone.

When the ramp was secure, Carole walked up it to get the horse. A pretty chestnut face with a white blaze turned toward her, ears pricked. In the dim light Carole couldn't really see what he looked like. What she could see was that no expense had been spared in shipping him down to Pine Hollow. The horse was resplendent in maroon and white, wearing every kind of bandage, boot, blanket, and head gear. In the stall next to him were a huge maroon-and-white tack trunk; two smaller trunks, also matching; and a number of grooming kits, buckets, and garment bags.

"Ready up there?"

"Ready!" Carole cried. She snapped a lead shank to the chestnut's halter and opened the stall door. As she did so, she glimpsed the nameplate gleaming on the leather cheek piece: Country Doctor.

"Okay, here we come!"

Taking care that he didn't rush (risking a scrape or injury), Carole led the gelding down the ramp to the driveway. He walked perfectly calmly until they got to the ground. Then he threw up his head and neighed loudly.

"That's right, boy. You're in your new home now," Carole murmured, stroking the glossy neck.

At the sound of the whinny, Stevie and Lisa emerged from the barn, followed by Red and then Max. Red whistled. "That is one good-looking horse," he remarked.

Stevie and Lisa looked at one another and laughed. Only at Pine Hollow would the men be so impressed by a beautiful horse. Still, the girls could see that Red was right. Even covered in his travel gear, the chestnut was a looker.

"What's his name?" Lisa asked.

"Says here, Country Doctor," Carole supplied.

"That must be his show name," Stevie guessed.

Carole nodded. "Yeah, we ought to give him a barn name, huh?" Most show horses went by short nicknames for easy reference.

"How about Doc?" Lisa suggested.

"Doc it is," Carole pronounced. She led the horse forward to stretch his legs.

"Hey, why don't we take some of this stuff off him," Stevie volunteered.

"Great," said Carole. She held the gelding steady

16

while Stevie and Lisa removed his blanket and shipping bandages. When they were done, Carole got her first real look at him. She drew her breath in sharply. Doc looked like . . . like her dream horse! He was a bright chestnut with four white socks, about fifteen and a half hands high. He looked both strong and elegant. "Wow," Carole said with a sigh. "He is beautiful."

Lisa glanced at Carole. "No more beautiful than Starlight," she reminded her.

"Of course not, Lisa," Carole said hurriedly. "But that's like comparing apples and oranges. This horse is a top-of-the-line junior hunter. He probably cost more than—well, more than we could imagine."

"Thousands?" Lisa asked.

Stevie grinned. "Thousands and thousands and *thousands*."

Their speculation was cut short by Max. "Lisa! Stevie! Can you two go help Red finish spreading the bedding for our new arrival? Carole, walk him a good half hour or so, so he can really stretch, okay?"

"Okay, Max!" Carole called, as Lisa and Stevie ran to help Red. "Come on, boy, time to work out the kinks," she murmured. She started walking down the long driveway.

"Mind if I join you?" a voice asked.

Carole turned. It was the driver of the van. "I should probably work out the kinks, too. I've got a long drive ahead of me."

"Where to next?" Carole asked politely as the man fell into step with her.

"I've got to pick up two horses in North Carolina and bring 'em over to Tennessee. One of them's a real handful. Not like this guy," said the driver.

Carole smiled. One of the things she loved most about riding was horse talk. There was nothing like swapping stories, one horsey person to another. "So this guy's a champion up north?" she inquired.

"You got that right. Owner's absolutely horse-crazy. Takes him to every show she can."

"She?" Carole repeated absently.

"Young girl—'bout your age. Been riding since she could walk."

Ignoring the last comment, Carole asked, "So she rides hunters, not equitation?"

Most horse shows offered hunter classes, which judged the horse's form, and equitation classes, which judged the rider's form. Carole had done some of each with Starlight.

"Both," said the driver. "And they win in both."

Carole felt like frowning, but she forced another smile. "I've done both, too," she said.

The driver looked at her. "You got your own horse?"

"Yup. He's a half-Thoroughbred mix named Starlight. I trained him myself. I—" Carole paused, embarrassed that she had started to brag.

Luckily, the man didn't seem to notice. "Good for you," he said. "Training a horse is a real test of horsemanship—more than any of this horse show business, if you ask me."

Carole glowed. *I'll bet Doc's owner can't say that she's trained a horse*, she thought. Then she stopped. Why was she comparing herself to Doc's owner, a girl she'd never met? Why did she feel as if they were already in competition?

After a second Carole recovered herself and walked forward beside the chestnut. To her relief, the driver had continued talking, oblivious to the thoughts that were running through her mind.

"Anyway, this horse ought to be a great addition to the stable, eh? Not to mention his rider . . ."

"Yes," Carole said tightly, "I'm sure they'll—they'll help our Pony Club teams a lot."

Carole and the van driver reached the end of the driveway, turned around, and headed back. At the stables, Max came out to thank the man again and give him directions back to the highway. Carole lingered for a couple of moments, letting Doc nibble at the grass outside the barn. She was glad that the gelding seemed happy and relaxed. As he grazed, she looked him over a second time. His conformation was truly striking: a sloping shoulder, a short back . . . Try as she could, Carole couldn't find a single fault. A twinge of guilt pricked at her conscience. Starlight was beautiful, too. And Starlight had excellent conformation. The only thing this horse had that Starlight didn't was a price tag. But that was because Carole's father had bought him for her when the horse was young and relatively unschooled. By now he was probably worth a lot more. . . .

"You guys seem to have hit it off," a voice observed.

Carole glanced up, startled. She felt as if Max had read her thoughts—thoughts she wasn't proud of. Since when did she care how much Starlight was worth? Why would she want to put a price tag on him?

"Who wouldn't hit it off with a horse like this?" she said lightly.

"You've got a point," Max agreed.

"So, I hear his rider is supposed to be very good," Carole remarked. She knew she ought to leave the subject alone, but she couldn't. A side of her that until now she hadn't known existed seemed to have taken over.

"You bet. I don't know how good, but I've heard

she's hot stuff. Her name's Andrea Barry." Max paused and smiled down at Carole. "And I have the feeling you and Andrea Barry are really going to hit it off. This girl might be just as horse-crazy as you."

"Great," Carole said, her voice flat. To cover up her lack of enthusiasm, she added, "I can't wait to meet her. When is she coming?"

"I'm not sure. I think her family was having some trouble with the move," Max replied. "Say, Carole, why don't you exercise this boy till Andrea arrives? It would be good for you to try another horse, and I'm sure you'd have fun with him."

"Great!" Carole said, only this time she meant it. Since her first look at Doc, she'd been itching to try him out.

It only made the opportunity sweeter when Max added, "You're one of the few students I feel comfortable entrusting a new horse with." Before she could thank him, Max said brusquely, "Red and the girls are set with the stall. Better bring him in before it gets too late."

Feeling ten times better, Carole led Doc inside. Now she felt silly. Why was she getting all bent out of shape because an expensive show horse had arrived at Pine Hollow? She, Carole Hanson, was still the number one junior rider at Pine Hollow. Max trusted her to ride Doc—*and* he was counting on her to bring the Silver Stirrups Trophy home to Pine Hollow.

Besides, for all she knew, Doc's owner would turn out to be another Veronica diAngelo. Veronica had a lot of money. She had an expensive, nearly perfect show horse, Go For Blue. And she had won a lot of ribbons in competitions. But, as Carole knew, Veronica won not because she was a *great* rider. Veronica won because she was a *decent* rider—okay, even a *good* rider—who owned a *great* horse. She didn't have to make do with a young horse, a green horse, a horse with bad habits, a horse that didn't like to jump, a "bad mover," or even a horse like Stevie's mare, Belle, who had a mind of her own. Veronica could just sit there on Danny (Go For Blue's barn name) and win ribbons. Of course, she usually lost her temper or messed up or figured out some other way to ruin her chances, Carole thought with a grin. And Andrea Barry might be just like that.

"Open sesame!" Stevie murmured, pulling back Doc's stall door.

While Doc nodded regally, Carole led him into his new quarters and unsnapped the lead shank from the halter. When a horse first arrived at Pine Hollow, Max liked to leave the halter on for a few nights, as a safety precaution.

22

"This place looks like the Ritz," Carole joked. Doc's stall was bedded deeply, and he'd been given a new salt block and new buckets.

"It should," said Lisa, panting slightly. "Red had us use about a hundred bags of shavings."

From the stall next door, Red replied, "Only a hundred? Boy, you guys got off easy. Usually I use a thousand for a new horse."

Lisa grinned sheepishly. One thing they'd all learned about Pine Hollow—and yet always seemed to forget—was that the stall walls were thin. "I guess everybody deserves the red-carpet treatment once!" she responded.

Carole gave the chestnut a good pat and joined the others outside the stall. "Judging from this guy's equipment, I think Country Doctor gets the red-carpet treatment all the time," she said. Gratified, Carole noted that she could make the comment without feeling jealous, simply as an observation.

"You mean the maroon-carpet treatment," Stevie corrected her. "Maroon and white."

Carole grinned. "You got me there."

Lisa looked puzzled.

"Have you seen the tack room?" Stevie asked. When Lisa shook her head, Stevie explained, "Let me just say that this is a rider who believes in color coordination. You just saw the travel gear, but even his tack trunks are maroon and white!"

Lisa nodded. She understood completely. "Do you think this is a case of the Veronica diAngelo syndrome?" she asked.

"You said it," said Stevie. "So far, they sure seem to have a lot in common."

Lisa giggled. "Yeah, I'll bet . . . like tack trunks, garment bags, brush boxes—"

Carole laughed along with her friends. "Now, now," she chided them. "We have to remember how good it will be for Horse Wise to have another good jumper on the team." Horse Wise was the name of the Pine Hollow chapter of the Pony Club. Stevie, Lisa, and Carole were all active members.

Stevie rolled her eyes. "It might not be worth it if we have to put up with another rider like Veronica," she said dryly.

"Stevie—" Lisa began warningly. Nobody liked Veronica, but Stevie was the girl's self-appointed archenemy.

"I know, I know, but making up for Veronica's bad horsemanship is about all one team can handle!" Stevie insisted.

"Not to mention her lack of team spirit," Carole put in. Veronica, as they all knew, only cared about one thing: winning. And she only cared about one person winning: herself. So, despite Danny's good breeding and her own riding skills, she often jeopardized the team's chances.

Lisa spoke up. "All right, all right. You guys are being dumb! We haven't even met this Andrea Barry yet and we're already writing her off as another Veronica! She might be nothing like Veronica. She might be nice and smart and a great rider. Who knows? We might even ask her to join The Saddle Club. She might be just as horse-crazy as—as you, Carole!" Lisa concluded in a rush. "Right?"

Carole started. *Just as horse-crazy as you.* Wasn't that what Max had said?

"Right, Carole?" Lisa prompted her.

With her eyes on the bright chestnut gelding, Carole nodded. "Sure, Lisa," she said quietly. "I guess there's always that possibility, too."

AN HOUR LATER, the girls had helped with the evening feeding and were gathering up their things from the locker room. "See you guys tomorrow?" Lisa said, stuffing dirty breeches into her backpack.

Stevie nodded, her expression thoughtful. "I just realized that we only have a few days to practice for the schooling show."

"Hey . . . you're right," said Carole after a minute. "And I told Max I would give Doc some exercise."

"Maybe that's good," Lisa suggested. "You'll have a little break from Starlight and come back refreshed."

"That's true. And it is only a schooling show," Carole said, thinking aloud.

"What, saving yourself for Briarwood?" Stevie teased.

"Yeah, right," said Carole. "I don't want to burn out before the *big* show." She tried to keep her voice light, as if she were joking, but her words came out more serious than she had meant them to.

"You? Burn out? That'll be the day," Lisa said, shaking her head. "Maybe when you're ninety-nine."

"Yeah, when you're ninety-nine and you've won every silver stirrups, silver saddle, silver noseband, silver anything trophy on the East Coast!" Stevie laughed.

Carole laughed, too, then looked serious again. "Say, you guys?" she began.

Stevie and Lisa turned expectantly.

"Do you really think . . ." Carole stopped. She couldn't finish the sentence that had formed in her mind: *Do you really think I'll win the trophy?*

Carole couldn't understand what had gotten into her. Only a truly self-centered person, only a bad friend—only a *Veronica*—would ask a question like that under the circumstances. Stevie and Lisa had already implied several times that they did think she would win it. To make them come right out and say it would be rude. Besides, Carole reminded herself, Stevie and Lisa were competing, too. They had every chance in the world to win the trophy themselves. It was only because they were such good friends with Carole that they didn't mind being beaten by her. For her to go and rub their noses in it . . .

"Do we really think what?" Lisa asked.

"Oh—well—" Carole chewed her lip. "I mean, what I meant was, have you had a chance to really think about what classes you're going to enter at Briarwood?" she finished lamely.

"No, but let's go check out the schedule now," Stevie suggested.

Carole agreed, but Lisa had to go. "I've got to go home and eat dinner. Or, actually, I've got to go home and set the table so the family can eat dinner."

Stevie's hazel eyes started to sparkle. Lisa took one look at them and began to shake her head. "Oh no you don't, Stevie Lake. You can't convince me to try to get out of this one. The last chore you had me skip completely backfired."

Stevie did her best to look innocent. "What do you mean, Lisa? Didn't I get you out of emptying the dishwasher?"

"Yeah, and you got me *into* weeding the garden for a week as punishment!" Lisa exclaimed. She glanced at her watch. "Shoot! I've got to run!"

Leaving Carole and Stevie to consult the class schedule, Lisa hurried toward the stable telephone to call her mother. She turned a corner and ran smack-dab into Red O'Malley.

"I was about to come find you," said Red. "I'm headed out toward your house and I thought I could give you a lift."

"Really?" said Lisa. "That would make my mother's day. She might even forgive me for being late to set the table."

Lisa about-faced and walked with Red to his truck, an old blue pickup. The truck was just like Red, Lisa thought: not flashy or showy, a little weathered, but totally reliable.

"Pretty cool news about Briarwood, huh?" Lisa said when they were settled and heading out of the parking lot.

"Very cool," Red agreed. "And I think you kids have a great chance this year. You're all riding well."

"I hope so," said Lisa modestly. "Last year was so embarrassing!"

"It wasn't that bad," Red insisted.

"Maybe not for you!" Lisa said. "You stayed behind at Pine Hollow, as I recall!"

Laughing, the two of them recounted The Saddle Club's previous outing at Briarwood. Stevie and Carole had done well, but Lisa had made the mistake of bringing Prancer before either of them was ready.

29

When Prancer, fresh from her life on the track, had acted up at the horse show, Lisa hadn't been able to control her.

The day had been a turning point for Lisa. She had learned that one of the most important responsibilities a rider has is knowing what she and her horse can handle, in or out of the show ring.

"I'm glad we have the schooling show this weekend to tune up," Lisa concluded.

"Me too," said Red.

They drove in silence for a couple of minutes. Then Lisa looked curiously at Red. "Wait, you mean you're glad that we'll be able to tune up?" she queried.

"Well . . . that, and—well, I'm just glad, I guess," Red said, his eyes on the road.

Lisa eyed him narrowly. Now she had to get to the bottom of this. "Do you mean you might *ride* in the schooling show?" she asked. It was a well-known fact at Pine Hollow that although Red was an excellent rider, he didn't like to compete. He preferred to stay backstage, grooming, coaching, and exercising the boarders' show horses for them.

"Yeah, I thought I might take Kismet in the adult jumper class," Red said offhandedly.

"Red!" Lisa shrieked. "That's great!" She could see

that Red was trying to look casual. But after a minute, he broke into a huge grin.

"Yeah, Max talked me into it," he said gruffly.

"And it's okay with Mrs. Murphy?" Lisa asked. Mrs. Murphy was Kismet's owner.

Red nodded. "She's going to be away this weekend, but she's riding him at Briarwood. So she was happy that he would have a good warm-up."

"Wow . . . ," Lisa said. She wished that Red would drive ninety miles an hour so she could get home and call Stevie and Carole and tell them the news. Sure, it was only a schooling show, but it was news all the same: Red O'Malley was breaking his own tradition of never competing. Just as quickly, Lisa had another thought. Why couldn't Red ride at Briarwood, too? Even if Kismet was taken, there must be another horse at Pine Hollow that wasn't. Carole would probably have some great ideas. "Red, listen—" Lisa started to say.

But Red had other ideas. He had evidently read her thoughts the way she had read Stevie's a few minutes before. He held up a hand. "Oh no you don't. You can hold it right there, Lisa. I can see your mind working a million miles an hour, and in another five minutes you'll have your two cronies on the case and the three of you will decide that I should be riding in the American Horse Show. So get one thing straight: I'm taking Kismet in one, maybe two classes at the Pine Hollow schooling show this weekend. And that's that. Got it?"

Lisa frowned. She wished Stevie were there. She would have had a reply for Red. Stevie had a reply for everyone. But Lisa couldn't think of anything clever to say. She decided to try the honest approach. "Look, Red, I don't know anything about the American Horse Show. But if you could get a horse, wouldn't you like to ride at Briarwood?"

There was the tiniest fraction of a pause before Red began to shake his head. "Lisa, I'm warning you . . ."

"It was just a hypothetical question," Lisa said happily. There, that sounded more Stevian.

"Okay, I would like to ride at Briarwood. But," he continued before Lisa could respond, "finding a suitable horse at this late date would be impossible. I'm certainly not going to take a horse that's not ready." He glanced at Lisa. "You should understand that!"

"Now, Red," Lisa protested, "be nice!"

A few minutes later, Red brought the truck to a stop in front of Lisa's house. "What do you look so happy about?" he asked suspiciously.

Lisa grinned. "I'm just happy to be home, Red," she

said. She got out and shut the door behind her. "Thanks for the lift."

Red shook his head again. "You're welcome—I think," he said grimly. But he flashed a smile before he drove off.

Lisa watched the truck disappear and then hurried up the path to her house. What an exciting afternoon! First the news about Briarwood, then Red's news about himself. And no matter what he said, Lisa had heard him hesitate when she asked him about riding at the bigger show. Lisa was a sharp observer of people. She knew that when a person hesitated, it meant he was undecided. Clearly, it was up to The Saddle Club to decide him.

AFTER DINNER, LISA sprinted for the telephone in the family room. "Don't forget you have to empty the dishwasher when it's done!" Mrs. Atwood called.

"I won't, Mom!" Lisa replied. As she dialed Carole's number, Lisa promised herself, for the hundredth time, that if she ever became a famous scientist, she was going to build a robot that did one task and one task only: empty the dishwasher!

Carole answered the phone sounding sleepy. Or maybe not exactly sleepy, Lisa thought. But if it wasn't tiredness that was making Carole's voice sound flat, then the only other thing it could be was lack of enthusiasm, and Lisa *knew* it wasn't that.

"You sound tired, Carole," Stevie said, when they had included her in the three-way call.

"Do I? I guess I am, a little," Carole replied. It was a white lie, but Carole didn't feel like getting into the truth. The truth was that for the first time in forever, Carole didn't really feel like talking to her two best friends on the phone. She knew they would probably want to talk about horses, and then they would want to talk about the new horse. She tried to focus on what Lisa was saying.

"So then Red gets a big smile on his face and tells me he's going to ride Kismet in the schooling show!" Lisa announced.

"He is!" Carole exclaimed. All at once, her mood shifted from tepid to highly interested. "That's wonderful!"

"Maybe he'll do really well and decide to ride in the Briarwood show, too!" Stevie cried.

Lisa chuckled. She could always trust her friends to think the way she did. Quickly she recapped the conversation. "I could just *tell* that Red would be interested in going to Briarwood, provided that (a) he does well this weekend, and (b) somebody—meaning us—finds him a horse."

"What's wrong with Kismet? Mrs. Murphy shows him all the time," said Carole.

"That's just it," Lisa explained. "She's taking him herself."

"Oh . . . so that leaves Red high and dry," said Carole.

"More like low and—and slow," Stevie felt compelled to point out. "Because without a horse, he's grounded."

"Stevie!" Lisa and Carole cried. They knew if they didn't stop Stevie's punning right away, she would get completely out of control.

"I'm sure if we racked our brains, we could think of some possibilities," Carole said.

"I was hoping you'd say that," said Lisa.

"Let's see . . ." Carole was quiet a moment, considering. "Red needs a decent-sized horse."

"A good jumper," said Lisa.

"With at least some horse-show experience," added Stevie.

Before long, the girls had come up with a composite of the perfect mount for Red. The only problem was, they couldn't come up with a horse to fit the bill. Every horse they named had at least one major strike against it. It was too green, or too dead, or its owner was overprotective. "The kind of owner that gives you a list ten pages long about how to treat their 'baby' when they go away for two days," Carole said.

Still, the girls were optimistic. "I'm sure we're just forgetting an obvious choice," Carole said. "We need a nice, solid, attractive horse. Heck, maybe the girl who owns Country Doctor won't show up for a couple of weeks and Max will let Red ride the wonder horse." The thought was very appealing to Carole.

"Somehow I doubt that," said Lisa. "If his owner is as serious about riding as she's supposed to be, I'll bet she'll get here as soon as she can—definitely in time for Briarwood."

"You're probably right," Carole said, in a noncommittal tone of voice.

"Say, what about Danny?" Stevie suggested. "With Red instead of Veronica on his back, that horse would think he died and went to heaven!"

"No such luck," said Carole. "I wanted to take him out the other day, but Veronica left strict orders that only a special German dressage trainer she hired for the time she's away can go near him."

"Typical," said Lisa.

"*Too* typical," Stevie added.

After a few more minutes of talk, the three of them sighed in unison. Red, more than anyone, deserved a good mount for Briarwood. He probably wasn't admitting that he wanted to go for just that reason: He didn't want people to feel sorry for him. And with his quiet, reserved personality, he wouldn't want to make waves at Pine Hollow.

"Lisa!" Mrs. Atwood called. "The cycle stopped!"

"Be there in two minutes, Mom!" Lisa called back. To Carole and Stevie she said, "Why doesn't my mother understand the cardinal rule of dishwasher emptying?"

"What, that you have to wait for the dishes to cool off before unloading them?" said Stevie.

"Exactly!" Lisa cried, thrilled that her friend understood.

"I'll tell you why," said Stevie. "It's simple. In order to get us to do all the chores, parents pretend that they work really hard, too. But it's a myth. None of them have emptied a dishwasher or set a table in *months*—maybe even *years*! They don't remember what it's like! They only pretend to. *Your* mom just slipped up, and *you* caught her."

"Yeah, but what good does it do me?" Lisa asked.

"I can't wait to hear this," Carole muttered.

Stevie laughed into the receiver. "Absolutely none at all, I'm afraid. It just confirms my theory."

After Lisa hung up, Stevie and Carole continued a discussion they'd started that afternoon about what

37

classes they were going to enter at Briarwood. The choice wasn't difficult for Carole. She would ride in the junior equitation and junior hunter classes. She and Starlight were good at both of them, capable of winning in each division. But for Stevie the choice was harder. Belle could jump very well, but she didn't have beautiful form over the fences. Likewise, Stevie was a confident, skilled rider, but her style was more slapdash than Carole's. Both Belle and Stevie preferred jumper classes to hunter and equitation classes. In jumper classes, the only thing that mattered was that the horse cleared all the fences within a time limit. Form didn't count at all.

"I've thought about it a lot," Stevie said, "and I don't want to bite off more than I can chew. Belle and I are going to stick with junior jumpers. That's what we're good at."

"But don't you want to challenge yourself, the way Max said, and try an equitation class?" Carole suggested.

"I don't think so," Stevie replied. "I think riding at Briarwood, which is such a big show, will be enough of a challenge. This way we'll have fun and we'll have a chance to do well, too."

"I guess so . . . ," Carole said. She was going to pursue the subject but decided against it. It had suddenly dawned on her that she felt exactly the same way as Stevie. She wanted to stick with what she knew and have a chance to do well—*very* well. Anything short of the trophy would be a disappointment.

After they had said their good-byes, Carole hung up the phone and doodled absently on a piece of paper. She knew Max would disapprove of their conversation, but why should he? What was so wrong about wanting to do well, to prove what you knew and show off what you were good at?

Carole looked down at the paper she was sketching on. She'd drawn a horse's head with a ribbon pinned to its bridle that said First Prize. Beside the head she'd drawn a girl in boots and breeches, smiling. Humming softly to herself, Carole added one last detail: a huge, silver trophy, shining in the sun.

CAROLE RACED TO Pine Hollow after school the next day. Having two horses to exercise made her feel like a professional rider. A little guiltily, she gave Starlight a carrot and a quick hug; then she went to Doc's stall. As she was tacking up the new arrival, Red appeared. He leaned over the door to say hello.

"Lisa told us the good news, Red," said Carole, inching the girth tighter.

Red smiled. "Somehow I knew she would."

"Why don't you take Kismet out now? With us?" Carole suggested. She thought it would be fun if Red joined The Saddle Club in a preshow schooling session.

But Red shook his head. "Can't. I was planning to, but Mrs. Murphy decided she wanted to have a private lesson with Max before she leaves for the week," he explained.

Carole couldn't help noticing his glum tone. It didn't seem fair that Red couldn't ride today, on this beautiful spring afternoon. *Here I have two horses to ride, and Red doesn't even have one,* Carole thought. She straightened up. What the heck was she thinking? "Say, Red? Would you like to ride Starlight today?"

Red's face lit up. "I'd love to, Carole. If you wouldn't mind."

"Mind? I'd love it! I was wondering all day how I would have time to ride two horses. This will be a huge help to me." Carole made sure she emphasized that Red was doing *her* a favor and not vice versa, so that Red wouldn't feel indebted to her.

Soon Red had the bay gelding ready. The two of them joined Carole and Doc at the mounting block. "Anything I should know, Carole?" Red asked, springing lightly onto Starlight's back.

Carole watched Red walk Starlight in a circle. It was strange seeing someone else riding her horse. She had to admit that Red looked good on him. Red sat easily in the saddle, the reins loose so that Starlight could stretch. Starlight looked perfectly relaxed. To her surprise, Carole felt a touch of disappointment. She had thought her horse might react more to the switch.

"Let's see . . . ," Carole said. "I can't really think of anything . . . Well . . . Well, okay—sometimes he's afraid of shadows. He shies, and you really have to sit firm and tighten the reins. And you don't want to let him jig at the walk. It's a bad habit, you know. And of course he tends to get faster on the long sides of the ring and slower on the short sides. And you'll notice he doesn't always bend into the corners. You really have to use your inside leg. And come to think of it, your outside leg, too, to keep his hindquarters in line. And don't forget—"

"Carole?" Red broke in. "I think I can handle it," he said gently.

Carole stopped, flustered. She was acting like one of those overprotective owners she always made fun of! She was giving Red a lot of unnecessary advice on how to ride Starlight. Red—who'd been riding since he was two! She laughed. "Sorry, I know you can."

Embarrassed, Carole mounted Doc. She caught up to Red and they walked to the outdoor ring together. Even at a walk, Doc had a long, swinging stride.

"How does he feel?" Red asked.

"Great!" said Carole. "A little higher and narrower than Starlight."

"Do you know anything about his training?" said Red.

Carole shook her head. "Not too much. Although I have the feeling this is going to be one easy ride—kind of like sitting in an armchair and holding the remote. He's probably been schooled within an inch of his life, like most fancy show horses."

As Carole finished her remark, a gust of wind shook the trees overhead. Before she could gather her reins, Doc shied violently and broke into a trot. Carole lost her stirrups and slid forward onto Doc's neck. "Ho! Ho, Doc. Ho, ho." In a moment she had recovered herself, but not before feeling stupid, angry at herself, and, for the second time, embarrassed in front of Red. She sat back and slowed Doc to a walk.

"He must be feeling a little fresh from his trip," Red said helpfully. "He'll work out of it."

"I know," Carole said shortly. She knew she sounded rude, but she couldn't handle advice right now. Luckily, they had reached the ring. A couple of other riders were working on the flat at the top of the ring. "I think I'll take him down to the end where it's quiet," Carole announced, thankful for the excuse to split up with Red.

She turned Doc away from Starlight. Doc dug in his toes and refused to move. Carole used her legs harder and pulled with her outside rein. Doc backed up two steps. Carole dug her heels into his barrel. Doc backed up two more steps. "You didn't bring a crop, did you, Red?" Carole said through clenched teeth.

"Nope. I knew you hardly ever used one on Starlight. Do you want me to go back and get one?" Red asked, his voice sympathetic.

"No! Never mind. I can do it." Using all her skill and strength, Carole turned the horse and forced him into a walk. Somehow she managed to get Doc, balking and fussing, down to the end of the ring. Then the real challenge began. As Carole knew, a lot of horses will test an unfamiliar rider to see what they can get away with. But Doc pulled out all the stops. He shied, he rushed forward, he threw in a buck. He tried to take off—twice. The most frustrating thing was that when he did settle down for five seconds, he had beautiful gaits. His trot was brisk, and his canter was round and slow. But the minute Carole let her reins get long or let herself get disorganized in any way, he put his head down and tried to buck.

Carole was concentrating so hard, and working so hard, that she didn't even notice when Lisa and Stevie (on Prancer and Belle) joined Red at the other end of the ring. Red called to Carole to ask if he could jump Starlight. "Fine! Fine! Do whatever you want!" Carole called back. She circled Doc, trotted into the middle of the ring, and brought him to a halt. Finally, the horse obeyed. Carole reached down and gave him a pat. Then she looked up. She saw Red, Lisa, and Stevie riding around a course of six small jumps. They were following each other like a hunt team. Red was leading, and he had Starlight in perfect form. Watching them, Carole felt left out. Starlight was behaving just as well with Red as he did with her. Doc shifted his weight from side to side, calling Carole's attention back to him.

Carole squared her shoulders in determination. "Okay, boy, let's get back out there. I think I may have figured you out."

As Carole asked for a walk, Doc pricked his ears up and turned his head. Carole saw a figure hurrying toward the ring. It was a girl about her age.

"Doc! Doc!" the girl cried. She ran pell-mell up to the ring and ducked under the fence. "Doc!"

Before Carole knew what had happened, the girl had her arms around Doc's neck. She was a thin girl with big brown eyes and long brown braids. "You must be Country Doctor's owner," Carole guessed.

The girl took a step back and beamed at Carole.

"That's right," she said breathlessly. "I'm Andrea Barry."

"So, you call him Doc, too," Carole observed. She felt as if Andrea had stolen The Saddle Club's nickname. But that was dumb: It was an obvious nickname—and, moreover, it was Andrea's horse.

"Yup. That's been his barn name for as long as I've had him," Andrea said. She stroked the chestnut neck, and Doc turned to nuzzle her shoulder.

"Max asked me to exercise him today. We didn't realize you'd be coming so soon," Carole explained, unable to keep the tone of disapproval out of her voice.

Andrea looked embarrassed. "I guess I should have called first," she said. "Our plans changed and we ended up getting in early this morning. I couldn't wait to see Doc, so I came right over to ride."

"Oh, I'll get right off," Carole said shortly.

Andrea blushed. "I—I didn't mean that you had to get off," she stammered.

"That's okay," said Carole. Feeling slightly foolish, she took her feet out of the stirrups and hopped off. *This is how Red must feel,* she thought, *when Mrs. Murphy shows up to ride the horse he's been schooling all week.*

As Carole hit the ground, Doc pranced away from

her. At the same time, Carole and Andrea reached for the bridle to steady him. "Here, you take him," said Carole, relinquishing the reins.

"Thanks," said Andrea.

"You're welcome," Carole said. She stood there awkwardly for a moment.

"And thanks for riding him. I really appreciate it."

"Oh, that's okay," said Carole. "I try to do whatever I can to help Max out," she added pointedly. If Andrea was as spoiled as Veronica, Carole figured, she'd probably never helped out at the barn where she boarded her horse. She probably thought horses came groomed and tacked up. But it couldn't hurt to start her thinking about the idea that people actually had to work to keep Doc's chestnut coat so shiny.

Andrea didn't seem to have heard what Carole said. She was too busy fussing over Doc—checking his girth, scratching underneath his jaw, rubbing his forehead. Finally she adjusted her stirrups and got on.

"He's pretty excited today," Carole warned her. "He's been—"

Andrea laughed. "Let me guess: bucking, shying, and backing up, right?"

Carole nodded hesitantly.

"Sorry. I should have warned Mr. Regnery that he always acts up after a long ride in the van."

"Right, I know—" Carole began, but Andrea continued, oblivious.

"He's very sensitive to new riders, too. When he plays around you have to sit tight and make sure that your hands are up, not resting on the pommel or his neck. The line from your elbow to your hands should be parallel to the ground, like this"—Andrea demonstrated—"and not sloping down. You don't want a break where your hands join the reins. It's actually harder on a horse's mouth to keep letting the reins slide. That's how you get a horse with a dead mouth that pulls."

Carole took a step back. She swallowed hard. "I . . ." She stopped. She couldn't think of a single thing to say. She was in utter shock over what had just happened. *She* had been given a lecture about riding. And by a girl who had arrived at Pine Hollow *five minutes ago.* Who the heck did Andrea Barry think she was?

"Listen, I . . . ," Carole began again. She still didn't know how to put it into words. How could she tell Andrea that she was the best junior rider at Pine Hollow? That Andrea ought to be listening to her—and would be, very, very soon?

Carole was saved by Stevie, Lisa, and Red's trotting up to join the two of them. "Hey, you must be An-

drea!" Stevie called. When everybody had been introduced, horses included, Stevie and Lisa said they'd
better walk Belle and Prancer to cool them off.

"And I should trot and canter—to cool *him* off,"
Andrea joked.

Everyone laughed, except for Carole. She barely
managed a smile. She watched the three of them head
back to the rail, talking animatedly. She couldn't wait
to get Stevie and Lisa alone and tell them the truth
about Andrea—that she was a stuck-up know-it-all.

"Do you want to ride, Carole?" Red asked.

Carole gave him a look of gratitude. He obviously
felt bad about riding Starlight now that she was horse-
less. "No, that's okay, Red. I'm happy just to watch,"
she lied.

"You sure?"

Carole nodded.

"All right. Thanks again."

Stevie and Lisa, Carole noticed, had been all too
ready to leave her grounded while they got to know
the new girl. Feeling sorry for herself, Carole went to
lean on the rail. She was actually looking forward to
watching Andrea struggle with Doc . . .

Fifteen minutes later, the only thing Carole was
looking forward to was going home. With Andrea
aboard, Doc was a different horse—a different, per-

fectly obedient horse. He walked, trotted, walked, cantered, walked, turned on the forehand, lengthened stride at the trot, and did two flying lead changes. "What a show-off," Carole muttered to herself.

All of a sudden she had had enough for the day—of Pine Hollow, of riding, of Stevie and Lisa, and especially of Andrea Barry and Country Doctor. Carole even felt betrayed by Starlight. Couldn't he have acted up just a tiny bit with Red? She knew she was being unreasonable, but it was the first truly bad day she'd had at the stables in a long, long time. She couldn't figure out what, exactly, had gone wrong, but she had an empty feeling in the pit of her stomach. Without saying good-bye to any of them, Carole left the ring and headed home.

"Isn't she great?" Lisa said. It was later that evening, and the girls were talking on the phone.

"Great, how?" Carole asked. She'd been praying the subject of Andrea wouldn't come up, but of course it had.

"Well, she seems nice and smart and she's obviously an excellent rider," Lisa gushed.

"Yeah. After you left, she gave me some tips on how to get Belle to bend around the corners," Stevie chimed in. "They really worked well."

"You mean she started lecturing you?" Carole said coldly.

"No, not exactly lecturing," said Stevie. She thought for a minute. "Andrea's . . . Andrea's like you, Carole. She gets so enthusiastic that she gets carried away."

"She *is* like you, Carole," Lisa agreed. "You should see the way she fusses over Doc."

"Oh," said Carole, her voice flat.

"That reminds me, Carole. Andrea's starting school with us next week," Lisa said. "So we'll have to watch out for her and be extra nice to her." Although a grade apart, Lisa and Carole both attended Willow Creek Junior High. Stevie, who was Carole's age, went to Fenton Hall, a private school.

"Is she in your grade or mine?" Carole asked. She hoped Andrea was in Lisa's class, a year above hers. That way she wouldn't have to see the new girl as often.

"Neither. She's a grade below you," said Lisa. "But we can still talk to her in the hall, and . . ."

Carole didn't hear the rest. She was stunned by Lisa's announcement: Andrea Barry was *younger* than she was. *She's younger and she's just as good as you,* Carole heard a voice inside her head say. But that couldn't be true, could it? After all, she'd only seen

51

Andrea ride for fifteen minutes. How could you tell anything in fifteen minutes?

And yet, the truth was, Carole was enough of a horsewoman to be able to tell a lot in fifteen minutes. It wasn't just that Andrea had been able to make Doc perform so well. He was her own horse, after all. It was more than that. The minute the girl had gotten on, Carole had known that she was good. She had a good position, she had confidence. She looked—as people had often said about Carole—as if she'd been riding her whole life. But this afternoon, at the back of her mind, Carole had told herself not to worry: No doubt, with all her successes in the show ring, the girl had a good year or two on Carole. But now that mental security blanket had been stripped away. Carole felt her head spinning. What did it all mean?

Lisa and Stevie chattered on, unaware that on her end of the line, the third Saddle Club member was a million miles away.

"Red looked amazing on Starlight, didn't he?"

"We just have to find him a horse for Briarwood."

"Yeah. He admitted to me that he wants to enter, but he swore me to secrecy."

"I wonder what Andrea's planning to enter."

"Is she going to ride in the schooling show?"

"She said it sounded like a lot of fun."

"I'm so glad she's not like Veronica."

"Me too. What a relief."

"Aren't you, Carole?"

There was a moment of silence. Stevie cleared her throat. "Carole? Uh, Carole?"

5

STEVIE WOKE UP singing on the day of the schooling show. It was a sunny Saturday. The school year was nearly over. All she had to do that day was ride in two classes, one on the flat and one over fences. Who could ask for anything more? She yanked a pair of reasonably clean breeches out of the closet and rooted around in her laundry pile to find a ratcatcher shirt. The pin for her choker was nowhere to be found, but that didn't worry her. She knew she could borrow one from Lisa—Lisa always had an extra. Stuffing a pair of gloves into her pocket, Stevie went downstairs to breakfast. She put away a large stack of pancakes, fought her three brothers for the bacon, and whistled and sang all the way to Pine Hollow.

LISA SET HER alarm for seven A.M. She didn't have to be at the stables till nine, but she always gave herself more than enough time to get ready. Sure, this was only a schooling show, but Lisa wanted Prancer to look her best. Or close to her best—nobody bothered to braid for a schooling show. For Briarwood, Lisa would get up at five A.M. to do Prancer's mane.

In keeping with the informal tone of the show, Max had decided that the riders didn't have to wear coats—just breeches and ratcatcher shirts. Lisa's clothes were hanging tidily in her closet. Her mother had ironed them a week before. Lisa slipped them into a garment bag. She would wear jeans and a T-shirt until she rode to keep her show outfit perfectly clean. Finally, she checked her horse show bag one more time: hair nets, knee-high stockings (for wearing under her tight boots), choker pin, *extra* choker pin (in case Stevie forgot hers), gloves, extra gloves, boot polish, sugar cubes. At breakfast Lisa drank some orange juice and had two bites of cereal. She never ate much on a horse show morning, even a schooling show morning: She was too nervous. When she was ready to go, Mrs. Atwood gave her a bag lunch, got the family car out of the garage, and drove her daughter to Pine Hollow, half an hour ahead of schedule.

"CAROLE! REVEILLE!" COLONEL Hanson called. "Eggs for breakfast!"

Carole rolled over. Why was her father waking her up so early? Then she remembered: the schooling show. She groaned inwardly. Normally a show morning would have made her jump out of bed. But today she pulled the covers over her head and closed her eyes. She had a bad feeling about the day.

"Scrambled or poached, honey?" Carole's father called from downstairs.

Carole thrust the covers back and sat up. "Poached, Dad!" To herself she muttered, "I feel scrambled enough already." She hadn't slept well at all. She had tossed and turned and had one bad dream after another.

At the foot of the bed, Carole's cat, Snowball, stretched luxuriously and squinted at her. "I wish I could stay in bed with you," Carole murmured, rubbing the cat's head as she stood up. What was the point of going to a stupid *schooling* show anyway? It didn't *prove* anything.

Carole let herself think bad thoughts as she brushed

her teeth and got dressed. She wore her second-best pair of breeches and an old but clean shirt. "I'll bet Andrea Barry shows up in spanking-new, superexpensive clothes, custom boots . . ." Then Carole remembered Starlight. He was waiting in his stall, not knowing what the day would bring. Carole had to shake off her bad attitude, if only for him. She had to go and ride and do her best. Her best would be good enough. At least, it always had been in the past.

PINE HOLLOW WAS abuzz with excitement. Young riders hurried to and fro, carrying tack, brushes, and hard hats. The show was divided into two broad divisions: under eighteen and eighteen and over. The juniors would ride in the morning; there would be a break for lunch, with a discussion led by the judge; and the adults would ride in the afternoon. To keep it simple, there were only two classes for each group: equitation over fences and equitation on the flat.

"Why couldn't Max have thrown in a jumper division?" Stevie complained. "Then Belle and I would have a chance."

Stevie, Lisa, and Carole were standing by the ring watching the first rider make a circle before jumping. By watching the first few rounds, they could find out if there was a problem area on the course—a fence or a combination of fences that was particularly tricky. Then they would know where to pay extra attention when their turns came. It was one of the advantages of riding in the second half of the rotation. All three of The Saddle Club girls had drawn spots late in the order.

"You do have a chance, Stevie," Lisa told her. "You have good equitation when you try."

Carole nodded in agreement. "Just make sure you keep your elbows in and don't let Belle get strong after the first jump."

Stevie nodded, listening. She and Lisa were used to getting advice from Carole at shows. They paid attention because it worked. Yesterday and this morning Stevie had noticed that Andrea seemed to have good pointers, too, from her years of showing. That reminded Stevie of one she wanted to share with the other two. "Andrea said it helps to think of the next jump when you're in the air over the one before it."

"That makes sense," said Lisa. "Preparation always saves you from—"

Carole didn't let her finish. "Obviously," she broke in scornfully. "What else would you be thinking of when you're jumping?"

Stevie grinned. "Oh, I don't know—bacon cheeseburgers and fries? How to get back at my brothers?"

"Or Monday's math test?" Lisa joked.

But Carole went on in a serious voice: "Preparation is everything in jumping. If you don't start thinking about fence two until after you've landed from fence one, you'll be halfway there before you can actually do anything. Then it'll probably be too late to make an adjustment, to shorten or lengthen stride, so, chances are, you'll end up meeting the jump at a bad position."

"Kind of like that?" Lisa asked, pointing.

Out on the course, Betsy Cavanaugh had put her horse into a fence so awkwardly that the horse ran out at the last minute. The girls watched as she circled and reapproached the jump, a vertical comprised of alternating red and white poles. This time the horse took the fence in stride.

"Exactly like that," Carole said. "The turn to the vertical is tight. I'll bet a lot of people make that mistake."

"Too bad. Otherwise it was a good round," Lisa commented.

Watching a few more riders made it clear that Carole was right. There was one more run-out at the vertical and a couple of close calls where the horse jumped but very awkwardly. Other than that, the course seemed to be fairly straightforward. After the fifth rider, Lisa went to warm up Prancer. Stevie left after the sixth rider. "Shouldn't you come, too, Carole?" Stevie asked. "You ride before me."

"I'll be there in two secs," said Carole distractedly. She watched another course. Then she really had to go if she wanted to give Starlight a proper warm-up. She turned away from the ring when, out of the corner of her eye, she glimpsed a bright chestnut horse waiting at the gate. Andrea Barry was on deck. A little voice inside Carole's head told her to keep walking, to march straight to Starlight's stall and get on. But she couldn't move. She just had to see Andrea go.

Before the new pair entered the ring, Carole stole a glance at Andrea's face. It was the picture of calm composure. Carole's heart sank as Andrea picked up a confident canter and rode toward the first fence, an inviting low brush. Doc pricked his ears, snapped up his legs, and they were over. They took the next several fences in near-perfect form. Then came the vertical. Carole crossed her fingers. It was an ugly thought, but she couldn't help herself: She was actually hoping Andrea would make a mistake.

Doc came out of the turn too fast. Andrea barely had time to steady him. He took off from too far back and made a flat jump, barely clearing the fence. Carole turned for the barn. Now she had the information she needed: Andrea was beatable.

Carole had to hurry. She led Starlight out from his stall, where she'd left him, fully tacked. She mounted and began a rushed warm-up, walking, trotting, cantering. Starlight felt alert—more than alert. He felt fresh. He wanted to take off after the cross rails Carole used as a warm-up fence.

Carole barely heard the "Good luck!" Lisa called to her as she headed over to the ring. Waiting on deck, Carole realized she'd forgotten to ask Lisa how her ride had gone. That made Carole feel bad. The Saddle Club always tried to encourage one another at shows. It was sort of an offshoot of one of the rules of the club that they had to be willing to help one another out in any situation. She would make it up to Lisa later. Right now, Carole thought, she had more important things to worry about—like winning the equitation over fences.

The rider before Carole jumped her last fence and came cantering to the end of the ring. The gate opened, the rider came out, and Carole went in.

She halted briefly, summoning all her powers of concentration. But she found she couldn't concentrate. The colors and the noises blurred. The fences seemed almost unreal. Carole jumped the first few of them on autopilot. She felt frozen in the saddle, posed like a doll in two-point position. Starlight saved her at the next two jumps. Then came an oxer in the middle of the ring. Dimly Carole remembered that the vertical was the fence after the oxer. "Prepare, prepare," she muttered to herself. There were three strides to the oxer, then two, then one. In the air over the fence, Carole had one thought. She had to beat Andrea. The fear that had been lurking at the back of her mind came rushing forward: She couldn't let Andrea Barry displace her as the best junior rider at Pine Hollow.

Starlight touched down after the oxer. He was headed for the barn. The barn was his home. His instinct was to keep going toward it. He felt full of energy. The short warm-up had barely taken the edge off. He lengthened stride, speeding down the straightaway.

With a shock, Carole came to her senses. The vertical lay directly to her left. Another second and it would be too late to turn. In a flash, Carole sat up as hard as she could. She raised her hands off Starlight's neck, where she'd allowed them to fall. And she wrenched Starlight around to the next fence. He made an awkward turn, bowing his shoulder out and falling heavily onto his forehand.

Starlight pulled at the bit. There was a jump ahead, but it wasn't directly in his path. It would be easy to run around it. But he felt his rider urging him toward the set of raised poles. He knew what she wanted him to do. And because this was the rider who had trained him, because he trusted her and had learned to do her bidding time and again, he obeyed this time, too. He let her head him toward the fence. In order to clear it, he had to get way underneath it and pop up over it. But he did it. Rather than run out or refuse, he made a difficult, unnatural jump. He did his best.

MAX HAD GOTTEN Jock Sawyer to judge the schooling show. Jock was an old friend of Max's. He was known for being both hard and fair. He was also known for making his decisions fast. Today was no different. Ten minutes after Stevie, the last rider, completed her course, Jock handed his judge's card to Mrs. Reg, who read the results over the PA system. As if it were a real horse show, Mrs. Reg read the full names of both horses and riders.

"In sixth place, Ms. Lisa Atwood riding Pine Hollow's own Prancer."

Lisa trotted into the ring, grinning widely. Sixth was better than she'd expected. She'd had trouble at two fences and had been on the wrong lead for a couple of strides. Max came forward and pinned a green ribbon on Prancer's bridle. That made Lisa's grin even bigger. "I didn't know you got ribbons, Max!"

"Naturally," said Max, flashing her a smile. "I can't have my winners going home empty-handed."

Fifth was taken by a boy who lived on a farm adjacent to Pine Hollow.

Polly Giacomin got fourth. Lisa clapped loudly and gave Polly the thumbs-up sign. On her brown gelding, Polly looked pleased as she joined the growing line of winners.

"In third place, Ms. Stephanie Lake aboard Belle!" Mrs. Reg announced.

"Yippee!" Stevie cried. She stuffed the candy bar she had been eating into her pocket and rode into the ring, patting Belle extravagantly.

Max came forward with the yellow ribbon. "You see? Equitation won't kill you," he murmured, his eyes twinkling.

Stevie smiled sheepishly. Although she wouldn't have admitted it, she was proud of herself. She had ridden well, following Andrea's (and Carole's) advice to prepare early for every fence.

Lisa was delighted at Stevie's third. She knew Carole would win or get second, so that meant The Saddle Club would each take home at least one ribbon apiece.

"In second place—" Mrs. Reg continued.

No, no, no, Carole prayed, waiting outside the ring.

Don't let me get second. First or—or nothing! Her hands tensed on the reins.

"Ms. Carole Hanson riding Starlight!"

Stevie and Lisa burst into applause. The other riders clapped loudly. "What happened?" Polly joked to Stevie. "Did Carole fall off?"

The girls laughed. Carole's equitation was so good that for her to get second was rare.

"We've got to kid her about this one," Stevie said.

But Lisa shook her head wordlessly. One look at her friend and she knew that the second was no laughing matter to Carole.

Stone-faced, Carole rode into the ring.

"Nice job except for the vertical," Max murmured. "But you know that."

Carole forced herself to turn her lips up politely. But she wasn't smiling. She couldn't. The red ribbon fluttering on Starlight's bridle made her face burn with shame. She glanced at the crowd. She was sure everyone was laughing at her. Her friends, Max, Mrs. Reg, the stable hands, the other local junior riders—didn't they see it? This wasn't just one class at a schooling show. It was much, much more. Carole's worst fear had come true: In front of everyone, she had lost her edge. She had gone from being the best to being second best. And she had been beaten by someone a year younger! How would she ever prove that she was better *now*?

"And in first place, winner of the junior equitation over fences, a newcomer to Pine Hollow, Ms. Andrea Barry riding Country Doctor!"

Carole couldn't watch. She kept her eyes on the ground.

"Hey, congratulations! Carole, right?"

"Yeah," said Carole. She couldn't look Andrea Barry in the face. "Congratulations to you, too." Her voice came out in a croak.

"That turn to the vertical was a bear!" Andrea said.

"I'll say!" Stevie chimed in. "I felt Belle's eyes pop when she realized she actually had to jump it."

Carole stared at Starlight's mane. She stared at the pommel of her saddle. She felt her throat tighten. It couldn't be, but it was: She was going to cry! She was not only a loser, but a poor loser as well! She was a bad sport!

"Your advice really helped," Stevie was saying. "What do you think I should do in the flat class if Belle falls into the circle?"

Carole could stand it no longer. "I—I have to go," she whispered. Her eyes blinded by tears, she spurred Starlight toward the barn.

Max stood up in front of the lunch crowd and waved his hands for silence. "Before we start the discussion, I'd like to thank my old friend, former master of fox-hounds, three-time member of the United States show jumping team, and veteran horse show judge Jock Sawyer. Jock took time out of his busy schedule to officiate at our little show today. Thanks again, Jock!"

The riders, clustered on the knoll behind the stable, clapped enthusiastically. This was one of the best parts of the schooling show, if not *the* best. After riding in the two classes, all the participants were invited to come to a lunchtime discussion with the judge. That way, they could learn from their mistakes. At "real" horse shows, riders were often left in the dark about the judge's decisions. Sometimes they could figure out why they had placed where they had; other times they had no idea what they'd done right or wrong.

"I just wish Carole could be here," Stevie whispered to Lisa.

"Look. There she is." Lisa gestured at Carole's approaching figure.

"Excellent!" Stevie said happily. She felt bad that Carole had missed the equitation on the flat class. At least now she would get to hear the talk. "Her stomachache must have gone away."

"Yeah," Lisa said noncommitally. "Maybe so." She squeezed closer to Stevie to make room for Carole.

"Feel better?" Stevie asked, as Carole sat down.

"A little," Carole said in a glum tone.

Lisa said nothing. She just gave Carole as welcoming a smile as she could. Somehow she had the feeling that Carole's stomachache was a topic to avoid.

Luckily, Jock Sawyer had stood up to address the riders. "First of all, I want to say that I've seen some excellent horsemanship this morning. You're a very promising bunch of junior riders. So congratulations to all of you. Now, we'll get to the jumping in a minute. But first a few quick comments about the flat class. Most of the mistakes I saw were pretty typical—forgetting to check leads and diagonals . . ."

As Jock reeled off the list of faults, Carole's face burned with shame. She was sure it had been completely obvious to everyone that she had copped out of the flat class—that she'd been too upset about getting second in the over-fences to continue. She'd made up the excuse of the stomachache, but she doubted she'd fooled anyone. Furtively, she scanned the crowd until she located Andrea Barry. The girl was sitting by herself near the top of the hill. Just the sight of her made Carole feel sick—with jealousy. According to Stevie and Lisa, nobody had even been close to her in the equitation on the flat.

"And now for the jumping. I saw many good rounds, but none was perfect." Jock paused and smiled for a moment. "I'll let you in on a secret: The red-and-white vertical doesn't bite!" A laugh went up from the crowd. "I'll let you in on another secret—and I'm being serious now. When I judge a show, I always like to have at least one fence like that. It separates the sheep from the goats. So, would anyone like to comment on the important elements of riding a tough course?"

"Preparation!" said a thin, clear voice.

Carole didn't even turn her head to look. Everybody else could hang on Andrea Barry's every word, but she wasn't going to.

"Right!" said Jock. "What's your name?"

"Andrea Barry."

"Oh, yes—you rode the chestnut. Nice horse."

"Thanks," said Andrea shyly.

"Do you want to explain exactly what you mean by preparation?" Jock asked.

"Sure," said Andrea. "Although I didn't exactly follow my own advice this morning," she admitted.

Stevie leaned toward Carole and Lisa. "She's so modest, isn't she?"

Lisa noticed that Carole was pretending not to hear. She tried to give Stevie a meaningful look, but Stevie had turned away. Sometimes Stevie could be so insensitive!

"Basically, you want your horse to be ready as early as possible for the next jump. You have to think about the next jump when you're in the air over the one before it. You can't wait until . . ."

Not this again! Carole listened miserably as Andrea rattled on. This was *her* job! *She* was the one who was supposed to answer the judge's questions! *She* was the one who was supposed to get complimented on her horse! Carole glanced imploringly at Max. He would

70

help her, wouldn't he? When Andrea finished, wouldn't he interrupt to ask for Carole's opinion?

". . . so that you meet the fence from the right spot," Andrea concluded.

"I couldn't have said it better myself," the judge agreed.

Carole fixed her eyes on Max, willing him to say something. Max straightened up from the fence he was leaning against. He cleared his throat. "Excuse me, Jock—" he began.

Carole took a breath.

"—but I want to reiterate what Andrea was saying. It's very important to . . ."

Carole put her head down. It was throbbing so hard it felt as if it would burst. This couldn't be happening.

". . . as Carole did."

At the sound of her name, Carole looked up.

Max and Jock Sawyer were looking at her.

"Huh?" Carole said.

"I was just wondering if you forgot where the vertical was located, relative to the oxer before it," Max said. "From my angle, it looked as if you really had to yank Starlight around."

Carole cringed at the word *yank*. She wished a hole would open up in the hill so that she could sink through it. Max was finally singling her out—to em-

71

barrass her even more! When Carole finally spoke, her voice was barely audible. "I—I guess my mind was on other things," she said unhappily. *One other thing*, she thought, *or rather, one other person.*

"Wandering mind disease," the judge joked. "It's something we all suffer from."

Carole tried to smile, but her face froze. Would the discussion never end?

Finally, after what seemed like hours, Max thanked the judge again. He invited all the junior riders to stay for the afternoon and watch the adults ride. A final round of applause broke out. Jock Sawyer had been a huge hit.

"Let's go help Red get ready and then get good seats to watch the jumping," said Stevie as they stood up.

"Sounds good," Lisa said.

They looked around for Carole. She was hurrying toward the driveway. Stevie put her hands to her mouth to call her back.

"I wouldn't," Lisa said. "Leave her be."

Stevie raised an eyebrow at Lisa. "Are you serious?"

Lisa nodded.

"Say, there's Andrea. Let's ask her to come along, too." Stevie waved the girl over. Then she turned back to Lisa. "Is there something going on that I don't know about?"

72

"Yes," Lisa said succinctly.

"But then—"

"I'll explain later," Lisa said as Andrea joined them.

Stevie shrugged. "Okay. Hey, Andrea, two firsts—congratulations!"

LATE IN THE AFTERNOON, the schooling show came to an end. The ribbons had been handed out, the horses untacked, walked, groomed, and fed. Lisa and Stevie were polishing their bridles in the tack room.

"Boy, I can't believe Carole missed seeing Red win equitation on the flat," Stevie said.

"And he would have done much better over fences if Kismet hadn't been such a pain," Lisa observed.

Stevie agreed. "That's the problem with riding other people's horses—you have to deal with all the bad habits they've developed from their owners." Stevie paused, soaping her reins. "So now can you tell me what's eating Carole?" she asked.

"I can try," Lisa began hesitantly. It was easy for her to understand what Carole was going through, but she wasn't sure how to make Stevie understand.

Lisa understood because she would have felt the same way if a new student had come to Willow Creek Junior High and started winning all the academic prizes. In school, Lisa was used to being number one.

She was very competitive when it came to grades. On the outside, Carole didn't seem competitive at all. She had a low-key attitude, she was always willing to help her friends and fellow competitors, and she loved riding for riding's sake, not just for the thrill of competition. But the bottom line was that she was used to being number one at Pine Hollow. It wasn't anything that was talked about; it was just understood. Now it looked as if Andrea Barry was going to give Carole a run for her money. Instead of taking it in stride and doing her best, Carole was freaking out. It didn't help that Andrea was a year younger. Lisa tried to put all this into words.

"I see what you're saying," Stevie agreed when Lisa had finished, "but I don't see why Carole would be so upset. It's not like Andrea's that much better—if she even *is* better. Carole could have beaten her today, and I'm sure she could beat her on another day. At Briarwood, maybe."

"Right. But Carole doesn't realize that. She's too busy panicking," said Lisa.

Stevie wanted to hear more, but the tack room door swung open and Andrea came in. "Hi," she said shyly. "I hope I'm not interrupting."

"Interrupting?" Stevie laughed. "Any time you want to 'interrupt' while I'm cleaning tack is fine by me!"

"On your way home?" Lisa asked. Andrea had changed into street clothes.

For some reason the question seemed to worry the new girl. "Yeah, I guess I'll go soon."

"Where do you live?" Stevie asked, to be friendly.

Andrea mumbled something incoherent.

"Where?" said Stevie.

"Flint Lane," Andrea repeated.

Stevie nodded. Flint Lane was way out on the outskirts of Willow Creek. "Your mom's picking you up?"

Looking down at the floor, Andrea shook her head. "No. I'm walking home," she said quietly.

Above her head, Stevie and Lisa exchanged glances. Nobody *walked* from Pine Hollow to Flint Lane.

Lisa spoke up. "I don't think that's a good idea, Andrea," she said gently. "You probably don't realize it, but your house is about six miles from here."

"Yeah, why don't you call your mom?" Stevie suggested. "We can give her directions."

Now Andrea looked extremely uncomfortable. "No, I think I'll walk," she said.

"But Andrea—" Stevie began.

"Look," Lisa broke in, "*my* mother is coming in five minutes. We can run you home, okay?"

"Oh, but I don't want you to go to any trouble—" Andrea began to protest.

"It's no trouble at all," Lisa said firmly. Then, prompted by Andrea's downcast face, she added, "Anyway, my mother loves to meet my new friends."

"Thanks, Lisa," Andrea murmured.

"Any time." Lisa picked up Prancer's bit from the bucket where it had been soaping and began to scrub it. She didn't want to look at Stevie, but she knew what they were both thinking: Andrea certainly wasn't acting like a girl who had just won two blue ribbons.

CAROLE LAY ON her bed, choking back sobs. *Two blue ribbons*, she thought. The phrase kept repeating itself in her head. Andrea Barry had everything. She was not only better *and* younger, she also had advantages Carole did not. She had parents who were willing to spend whatever it took to help her get ahead. With a stab of jealousy, Carole remembered the fancy matching brush boxes, tack trunks, garment bags. Carole's parents—her father and her mother, when she was alive—had always supported her riding, too. But her parents weren't rich. And even if they had been rich, Carole realized, her father wouldn't have wanted her to have all the stuff Andrea did. Colonel Hanson believed in using hard work and elbow grease to get ahead.

All at once, the tears that had been brimming in her eyes spilled over and streamed down Carole's face. How could she compete with a girl who had been given everything?

Colonel Hanson rapped on the door and stuck his head in. "Stomachache any better?" he inquired. " 'Cause dinner's almost ready."

"Uh . . . yeah, Dad," Carole said, wiping at her tears.

Carole's father withdrew from the room but then stepped back in. "It's not really a stomachache that's got you down, is it, honey?" he asked gently.

Carole shook her head.

"Did something happen at the schooling show?" Colonel Hanson guessed.

Sniffing hard, Carole nodded.

"Can you tell me about it?" her father asked quietly. He came and sat on the edge of her bed.

Carole swallowed. "It was awful, Dad. I—I messed up. And then I dropped out," she admitted.

Colonel Hanson nodded, his face serious. "I'm sorry, sweetheart. But everybody messes up some-times—nobody's perfect, you know."

"I know, Dad," Carole said quietly. "But I shouldn't have dropped out, should I?"

Colonel Hanson put an arm around her shoulders. "What do you think, honey?"

Carole could barely respond. The truth was, she was not only jealous of Andrea, she was embarrassed at what she'd done. "I know I shouldn't have, but you see . . ." Slowly, haltingly, Carole heard herself telling her father about Andrea Barry, what a great rider she was, how nice her horse was, et cetera. "She—she's *perfect*, Dad! She has everything!"

Colonel Hanson listened without interrupting. "I have a suggestion," he said when Carole had finished.

"Yes, Dad? What do you think I should do?"

Colonel Hanson's eyes twinkled. "The first thing I think you should do is try to get up and come down to dinner. We're having turkey burgers."

Carole smiled a little in spite of herself. Trust her father to think that food would cheer her up.

Then he continued more seriously. "And as for Andrea Barry, who's to say you won't beat her the next time? Or the time after that? A little competition can be a good thing, I always say. It keeps you on your toes, right, honey?"

"I—I guess so, Dad," Carole said doubtfully.

Colonel Hanson gave her shoulders a squeeze. "You

might surprise yourself," he suggested. "You might find it's actually *more* fun having some friendly rivalry at Pine Hollow."

Carole smiled wanly. How could she admit to her father that she didn't *want* a rival? That she had been perfectly happy being number one all by herself?

"Now, how's that stomachache?" Colonel Hanson asked.

"It's better, Dad," Carole said quickly. "Thanks."

"There's my girl," he said, standing up. "And how about those burgers? Provided they're not burned to a crisp, that is."

Carole managed a laugh. "Sure, Dad. Turkey burgers sound great. I'll be down in five."

After her father left, Carole got up, went to the bathroom, and splashed water on her face. For a minute she felt like crying again, but she gritted her teeth instead. "Dad's right," she murmured to her reflection in the mirror. "Competition *can* be good." She had to believe that, or she would keep feeling sorry for herself—and that meant feeling miserable.

And as Carole combed her hair and went down the stairs, her self-pity seeped away and was replaced with a new determination: a die-hard determination to beat Andrea at Briarwood, no matter what. To prove, once and for all, that she, Carole Hanson, was the undisputed best junior rider in the region. And there was only one way to do that: to win the Silver Stirrups Trophy.

As LISA HAD PREDICTED, her mother was happy to drive Andrea home. In the car, Andrea was quiet, so Lisa chatted happily about the show. She mentioned Andrea's two firsts, as well as her own sixth in jumping. Lisa had also gotten a third on the flat. With Carole sitting out and Stevie riding sloppily, Lisa had been the only member of The Saddle Club to place in the second class.

"Congratulations, dear," said Mrs. Atwood. "And congratulations to you, Andrea," she added, clearly impressed.

"Thank you," Andrea said softly.

"You must have ridden exceptionally well to beat Carole Hanson. She's a wonderful rider," Mrs. Atwood remarked. She, like the other Pine Hollow parents, was used to hearing about Carole's successes.

"Mom!" Lisa whispered, mortified.

"Oh, that's okay," said Andrea. "I was surprised I beat Carole in the first class, too. Everybody has told me how good she is. I'm sure the only reason I won was that she wasn't feeling well."

"Lisa tells me that you're starting at the junior

high," Mrs. Atwood continued. "I think you'll find it's an excellent school."

"My mom has to say that," Lisa said apologetically. "She's the head of the P.T.A."

Andrea didn't seem to find the joke funny. She stared straight ahead, barely nodding.

Mrs. Atwood gave Lisa a reproving look. "Do you think your mother or father would like to join the P.T.A.?"

Andrea opened her mouth, then seemed to hesitate. "I—"

"It's not a big time commitment," Mrs. Atwood pressed on. "We have meetings once a month. In fact, there's one this coming Wednesday. Why don't I give your mother a call?"

"No! Don't do that!" Andrea cried.

Mrs. Atwood turned her head around in surprise.

"My mother's dead!" Andrea blurted out.

Lisa gulped for air. She could hardly believe what Andrea had just said. She could see her mother was at a loss for words, too. Mrs. Atwood pulled over to the side of the road and stopped the car. She turned to Andrea. Finally, she spoke. "Andrea, I'm so terribly sorry. I had no idea."

"I know. I never know how to tell anyone," Andrea said in a whisper.

81

"When did she die?" Mrs. Atwood asked gently.

"A year ago," Andrea said. "She—she was in a car accident. It was the middle of winter, and the streets were icy."

Mrs. Atwood put a comforting hand on Andrea's. After a few minutes of silence, she started the car and drove on. Lisa felt like an idiot. She still couldn't think of anything to say. She felt so sorry for Andrea! The only person who would understand what Andrea had gone through was Carole. Carole had lost her mother to cancer a few years before. Lisa was in such a daze that she hardly knew when they pulled up outside Andrea's house. She looked out the window. The house was small and dark. It didn't look as if anyone was home.

"I hate to leave you alone, dear," Mrs. Atwood said. "Why don't you come to our house for dinner?"

Lisa felt a rush of gratitude toward her mother for being so nice.

"No—no, thank you. I'm used to coming home alone," Andrea said. "See?" She reached underneath her shirt and pulled out a key on a ribbon. "I can let myself in."

Despite Mrs. Atwood's arguments, Andrea seemed determined to stay by herself. Lisa and her mother watched from the car as she walked up to the house and disappeared through the front door. In a minute or two, a light went on inside and they saw Andrea wave.

As they drove home, Lisa was silent. She couldn't begin to sort through all she'd learned about Andrea Barry in the past ten minutes. Here she had assumed Andrea was a rich, happy-go-lucky girl with nothing to worry about other than where the next blue ribbon was coming from. "It's funny, her house was a lot smaller than I would have guessed," Lisa mused aloud.

Mrs. Atwood eyed her sharply. "What's that supposed to mean?"

Snapping to attention, Lisa realized how bad her comment must have sounded. She hastened to explain. "It's just that—well, her horse—and all her riding stuff is so nice that I thought—"

"That's a thought you may want to keep to yourself," Mrs. Atwood said.

"But—" Lisa started to say.

"Families spend their money on different things," Mrs. Atwood rebuked her. "It's not your business to ask why."

At home, Mrs. Atwood told Lisa to call Andrea to make sure she was all right. Lisa was glad to obey. She called Information, got the Barrys' number, and dialed it. Andrea answered in a muted voice.

"Andrea? It's Lisa. We just wanted to make sure you were—you were—" Lisa faltered. Of course Andrea wasn't *okay*. Who could be okay when her mother had died a year ago? "Umm, I just called to say hi and welcome you to Pine Hollow again."

"Thanks, Lisa. And listen, please don't tell anyone about my mom, okay? I don't want people to feel sorry for me."

"But I—"

Once again Lisa's protests were cut short. "I have to go. My dad came home and he's trying to go to sleep. I'll talk to you later. Bye."

With that, Andrea hung up, and the silence of the dead air filled Lisa's ear.

AFTER THE HUBBUB of the schooling show, Pine Hollow seemed unusually quiet on Sunday. The Saddle Club had agreed to meet in the afternoon. They weren't planning to ride, but there was plenty of other stuff they could do to get ready for Briarwood, which was now less than a week away.

This was the part of riding that Stevie was less than keen on. She just couldn't get as excited as Carole about rolling leg bandages and clipping the hair in Belle's ears. On the other hand, Stevie thought, heading into the tack room, she also didn't get as worked up as Carole did about being the best.

Stevie had thought a lot about what Lisa had said,

and she thought she was right: Carole was jealous of Andrea. What Stevie didn't understand was why it mattered who was number one. Why did Carole and Lisa *care* so much? Why didn't they realize that the important thing in life was to have fun?

Inside, the tack room was the picture of Atwood organization. Lisa had arrived early and posted lists of everything they would need at the show. Beside each item she had put one of their names to show who was responsible for doing what. Stevie looked at the first item on the first list.

> *Leg bandages . . . Stevie*
> *(Get from storage room, roll, and stow four in each rider's tack box.)*

With a sigh, Stevie went to get the long cotton wraps from the storage space above the tack room. Before loading the horses into the Pine Hollow van, the girls would wrap their legs for protection. But the bandages themselves had to be rolled first so that they could be unrolled around the horses' legs. Picking up the first one and smoothing it out on her lap, Stevie went to work.

"Hey, you actually read my list!" Lisa exclaimed. She came in and shut the door behind her.

"Of course! Why wouldn't I? When have I ever deviated from authority?" Stevie demanded, in mock seriousness.

"If I answered that question completely, we'd still be standing here next week and we'd miss Briarwood," Lisa responded, not missing a beat.

Stevie flashed her a grin. "Speaking of missing Briarwood, I wish Red didn't have to."

"Did someone mention Briarwood?" Stevie and Lisa turned.

It was Carole. She had come early, too, to give Starlight a once-over. She was hoping that her new attitude would show clearly. There would be no more feeling sorry for herself—only pure determination to win the following weekend.

"Yeah. We were just saying that it's too bad Red doesn't have a horse for Briarwood," Stevie said.

"Oh," said Carole. She didn't have time to feel sorry for Red now, either. If he wanted a horse badly enough, he would find one.

"It's strange," Lisa said, making a few check marks on the lists, "but there's no one for him to ride. Max has school horses—they're *too* quiet. He has young horses—they're not ready. He has ponies—they're too small. But he doesn't have a nice, big, talented, trained horse who can jump."

"What about the boarders?" Carole asked impatiently. "Can't one of them lend Red a horse?"

Lisa stopped what she was doing and looked at Carole. She was surprised by Carole's tone of voice. "They could, but Red doesn't want to ask. And anyway, Kismet is the best."

"Then the best isn't great," Stevie remarked, "judging from the trouble he gave Red yesterday."

"If only there were another Starlight in the barn," Lisa said wistfully.

"Well, there isn't," Carole said flatly.

Lisa looked hard at Carole. Did Carole think she'd been hinting? She would never even have mentioned Starlight if she'd thought twice. She knew how important Briarwood was to Carole. "Carole, I wasn't suggesting—"

"Good," Carole said. She folded her arms across her chest. "Then don't. Because even one extra class could jeopardize Starlight's performance."

After a pause, Lisa said, her voice cold, "I know that."

Carole wasn't so sure she did. What did Lisa expect—that she would sit back and let Andrea win the trophy? Because that was exactly what would happen if Starlight got strung out from being shuffled back and forth between riders.

"Guys?" Stevie said with a wan smile. "Don't you think we ought to get started on these lists? We've got a lot to do before Saturday."

Stevie's attempt to change the subject didn't fool anyone, but both Carole and Lisa were glad to take her suggestion. They worked quietly for fifteen or twenty minutes, checking things off the first list, such as *Find horse show saddle pads* and *Mix fly spray and fill spray bottles*. Things almost seemed back to normal. Then Andrea Barry appeared.

Lisa greeted her warmly, praying that Carole would follow suit. "Do you want to help us get organized for the show?" she asked. That would be a perfect way for Andrea to get to know Stevie and Carole in a non-competitive environment.

But Andrea looked uncertain. "Are you going to be here in an hour? No, wait—in two hours?"

"I don't know. It's hard to say how long it will take us," Lisa replied. She was very conscious that Carole was listening. She wished Andrea would agree to help, even for half an hour. Otherwise, Lisa knew, she would come off sounding like a spoiled brat.

"Well, I'd love to help, but I have a lesson in fifteen minutes," Andrea explained.

"A lesson?" Lisa said, not comprehending.

"Yes—a lesson with Max," Andrea said.

89

Stevie jumped in to help sort things out. "We have lessons on Wednesdays," she informed Andrea. "Unless you're talking about Horse Wise—Pony Club, I mean. Those lessons are on Saturdays."

Now Andrea looked truly uncomfortable. "I—I know. This is a—a private lesson."

"Wow! You're taking a private lesson with Max?" Stevie said enthusiastically. "That's great!"

Sounding relieved, Andrea explained that she was used to having private lessons at home. "I thought I might as well try to keep to the same schedule as much as possible—at least until Briarwood," she added.

"Good idea," Stevie said generously. It was rare, but not unheard of, for young riders to take an occasional private lesson at Pine Hollow. More often than not, it was to work on a specific problem. But if Andrea came from a fancy show barn, Stevie knew, she was probably used to private lessons all the time.

Lisa glanced at Carole to see how she was taking the news, but Carole's back was turned. She seemed intent on her tack.

"Have a great ride," Lisa said, "and maybe you can help us later on this week."

Andrea frowned. "I hope so, but I'm pretty busy just getting myself ready."

Lisa pursed her lips. That wasn't the response she'd been hoping for. Then she remembered Andrea's situation at home. That could make it hard for her to hang out the way the rest of them did. "All right. Well, bye," she said awkwardly.

"Bye."

After Andrea had left, Carole turned around.

Lisa waited for her to say something negative.

"What?" Carole said. "If you're expecting me to be jealous of her, I'm not. She can have ten private lessons a day, for all I care."

Lisa noticed that there was a steely edge to Carole's voice.

"I'll still beat her next weekend. Her life may be perfect, and she may have everything that money can buy, but I'll still beat her."

"There's the spirit, Carole!" said Stevie.

Lisa remained quiet for a moment. Then she said, "You know, Carole, Andrea's life isn't as perfect as you think."

"Oh, really? What, she got a second place once?" Carole could hear how sarcastic she sounded, but she didn't care. She was not going to let Andrea Barry make her feel second best.

"No," said Lisa. "It's something very serious."

"What?" said Stevie, all ears.

91

"I can't tell anyone. I promised not to," Lisa replied. If only there were some way she could make Carole understand that Andrea was dealing with a lot more than equitation over fences. But she couldn't go back on her word. That would be a betrayal of Andrea.

"Look, let's just drop the subject, okay?" Carole said. The last thing she wanted was to get in a fight with one of her best friends about her new rival. It would be a huge waste of time and energy before Briarwood.

"Okay," said Lisa.

WORKING STEADILY FOR an hour, Lisa, Stevie, and Carole managed to check off almost the entire list. Some things they wouldn't do until closer to the show, such as polishing their boots. Feeling incredibly virtuous, Stevie suggested they adjourn to TD's for a treat. TD's was the local ice cream parlor and a favorite meeting spot for the girls. "We definitely deserve it. After all this work and no riding," Stevie said.

"Count me in!" said Lisa, giving a final sweep to the tack room.

"Carole?"

"I wish I could come, but I want to lunge Starlight. Maybe I'll meet you there later." The night before, Carole had promised herself that nothing, but nothing, was going to get in the way of her final week of preparation. That included trips to TD's.

Lisa and Stevie were disappointed, but they set off alone, urging Carole to hurry and try to join them there. When they were gone, Carole took a lunge line and lunge whip and went to get Starlight. On the way to his stall, she passed the indoor ring. She could hear Max instructing Andrea.

"Good. Good. Now bring him down to a walk."

Carole peeked into the ring.

"And tr-rot!" Max commanded.

Andrea leaned forward the slightest bit as Doc moved fluidly into the faster gait.

"Fine."

Carole glanced at Max's face. It was glowing with approval. "You ride this nicely on Saturday, you'll have the judges eating out of your hand," said Max.

Carole felt yesterday's jealousy hit her like a brick. Max had found himself a new star pupil!

It was funny, though: Andrea didn't look very happy. Her expression showed confusion—nervousness, even. "You really think so?" Andrea asked.

As they moved around the ring, Carole slipped away toward Starlight's stall. *"You really think so?"* she mimicked in a whining voice. "Just wait till Saturday," Carole said. "I'll show you exactly what I think!"

THE SADDLE CLUB had gotten TD's down to a routine. They always sat in the same booth. Stevie always ordered a disgusting-sounding sundae. And they always seemed to get the same grumpy waitress. When anything changed that routine, it didn't feel right. Today, two things were off. One was that Carole weren't with them. Minus a third of The Saddle Club, Stevie and Lisa felt like a skeleton crew. As if that weren't enough, the rude waitress was nowhere to be seen. Instead a polite older man came to take their order.

"Good afternoon," the man said. "What can I get you today?"

Lisa and Stevie looked at one another in surprise. Common courtesy? At TD's? They were so surprised, they forgot their orders.

"Have you girls been riding?" the waiter continued.

Lisa found her voice first. "Uh, sort of. How'd you guess?"

The man pointed to his nose. "Sensitive sense of smell—at least when it comes to horses."

Stevie and Lisa grinned sheepishly. They were used to hearing their friends, parents, and siblings complain about the horsey smell that clung to them after Pine Hollow afternoons. Luckily, the waiter didn't seem annoyed. "Shall I come back in a few minutes?" he inquired.

"Oh, no—I think we're ready. I'll have a small chocolate chip on a sugar cone with sprinkles," Lisa said.

"And for you, miss?"

Stevie thought for a minute. "A strawberry sundae on coffee ice cream with caramel and blueberry toppings, marshmallow, and two cherries," she said. Both she and Lisa glanced up at the waiter, expecting him to show some reaction to the unusual order.

"Very good, miss," said the man. He jotted it down and left the table.

Stevie watched him return to the counter, her curiosity piqued. "He seems too polite to be working here," she observed.

"Yeah. Strange, isn't it?" Lisa said.

When the man returned with their orders, something about his manner seemed almost sad to Stevie. To be friendly, she asked if he ever rode.

The waiter smiled. "Not anymore," he said ruefully. "Not since my wife died last year. She and I used to ride together, and, well . . ." His voice drifted off momentarily.

Stevie shifted in her seat, sorry that she'd touched on such a sensitive topic.

"But my daughter rides," the man continued. "When she lost her mother, she threw herself into the sport." The man sighed. "Sometimes I wonder if it makes Andrea happy, though . . ."

Andrea? Lisa thought.

"Andrea!" Stevie exclaimed. "You don't mean Andrea Barry, do you?"

The man turned his attention to Stevie at once. "Why, yes—yes, I do. Do you know my daughter?"

"We just met her. We ride at Pine Hollow," Stevie explained as she and Lisa introduced themselves.

"How wonderful! I was worried there wouldn't be anyone Andrea's age," said Mr. Barry, looking pleased.

96

"Oh, there are lots of junior-high kids at Pine Hollow," Stevie informed him. "We hang out at the barn all the time."

"I'm so glad to hear that," Mr. Barry said. "Riding is Andrea's whole life, so it might be hard for her to make friends at school." He sighed again. "I know this move has been hard on her."

"Why did you move?" Stevie asked.

"Stevie!" Lisa whispered, kicking her under the table. Lisa was appalled. Sometimes Stevie's nosiness was really out of control.

But Mr. Barry seemed glad to talk. "I got transferred. I could either stay and keep the job I had for less pay, or move down here and make a little more. Staying would have meant selling Doc. And I could never do that to Andrea. He's all she has, really . . ."

"You mean, Tastee Delight transfers people?" Stevie asked. "Wow, I didn't know working at an ice cream parlor was that—"

This time Lisa's kick hit home. "Ow!" Stevie said, wincing.

But her comment had actually brought a smile to Mr. Barry's lips. "This is just my weekend job," he said, laughing. "I'm a computer salesman during the week. It's harder than it used to be to make ends meet. Of course, I'm not complaining. I'd do anything to make Andrea happy. And speaking of jobs, I ought to get back to work. But I'm very glad to have met you both. And enjoy your ice cream, all right?"

Stevie and Lisa waited until Mr. Barry had gone back behind the counter. Then they began talking in hushed tones. Now that Stevie knew that Mrs. Barry had died, Lisa could express how sorry she was for Andrea. Stevie sympathized immediately. So much was clear now. Stevie knew Andrea must still be devastated about her mother. And moving only a year afterward must have been traumatic, to say the least. It was no wonder riding was Andrea's "whole life." But there was another element of the story that both Stevie and Lisa had picked up on: The Barrys were far from rich. Mr. Barry was working two jobs to pay for Andrea's riding. Haltingly, Lisa described the scene at Andrea's house the night before.

"So nobody was home to let her in?" said Stevie. "On a Saturday night?"

Lisa nodded. "And when I called a half hour later, her dad had come home and gone right to bed."

Stevie let out a long breath. "I wish I'd known. I would have invited her to my house for the night." Saturday nights at the Lakes' were always fun. Stevie's parents would cook dinner for her and her three brothers and then they would watch TV together or play games. Stevie couldn't imagine coming home to a dark, empty house.

"The sad thing is, it probably puts a lot of pressure on Andrea, knowing her dad is sacrificing so much for her," Lisa pointed out.

"Gee, I'll bet you're right," Stevie said. "I never thought of that."

The girls ate in silence for a few moments. Then Stevie said, "Obviously, there's only one thing to do."

"What?" Lisa asked, though she was fairly certain she knew what Stevie was going to say.

"Simple: make helping Andrea a Saddle Club project," Stevie replied. "We can't make her life perfect, but at least we can be her friends."

"Right. But what about the fact that the Saddle Club member we need most thinks Andrea has a perfect life already?"

"Yeah, but Carole will change her mind once she hears about Andrea's mother," Stevie said.

"I guess so," Lisa said tentatively.

Stevie raised her eyebrows. "You sound skeptical."

"I did promise Andrea I wouldn't say anything," Lisa said.

"Right. And you didn't."

"But what if Carole said something and—"

"Carole's not going to say anything. But if she

knows what Andrea's been through—and is still going through—she won't be as competitive with her."

Lisa didn't respond right away. She couldn't put her finger on it, but there still seemed something wrong about calling up Carole and telling her very private details about Andrea's life. Lisa tried to imagine the conversation: *Hi, Carole? Lisa and Stevie. We just wanted you to know that Andrea's mother died a year ago and the Barrys don't have much money.*

And what if it backfired? What if Carole thought they were trying to force her to be friends with Andrea out of pity? Or that they were suggesting that Carole not try her best at Briarwood? Carole was so hypersensitive about the Silver Stirrups Trophy right now that she really wasn't herself. There was no telling how she would react.

Lisa voiced some of her doubts to Stevie, but Stevie still thought they should tell Carole what they'd learned.

"If only Carole had been here!" Lisa wished aloud.

"I know." Stevie glanced at the clock on the wall. "I guess she's not coming, huh?"

"No. She would have been here by now," Lisa said. "I'll bet she stayed at the barn all afternoon."

Before Stevie could respond, Andrea's father appeared at the booth. "Can I get you anything else?" he inquired.

Lisa and Stevie shook their heads. They both felt a little guilty about the discussion they'd been having. "No thanks!" they said in unison.

"All right then, here's the check. Have a good day, girls."

Normally The Saddle Club were fair but not big tippers. Today, however, both Lisa and Stevie tipped generously. They smiled when they realized they'd had the same idea.

"Oats for Country Doctor?" Lisa inquired, pointing at Stevie's pile of quarters.

Stevie shook her head. "Entry fees for Andrea."

IT WAS STILL early, so Stevie and Lisa decided to sit in the sun for a while. Lisa thought they ought to discuss the other Saddle Club project.

"What's there to discuss?" Stevie said glumly. "The show's a week away and Red doesn't have a horse."

Lisa had to admit that Stevie was right. She had racked her brains, but for the life of her she could not come up with an appropriate mount. "I keep thinking about how excited Red looked yesterday when he got his ribbon," she said.

"Heck, he even looked excited when Kismet acted up and he got two refusals," said Stevie. "I think he's finally realized how much he's been missing by not showing."

"And now he's going to keep missing it," Lisa remarked.

None of the stores the girls visited cheered them up, so a half hour later they left the shopping center, despondent instead of psyched as they normally were after a trip to TD's. "This time next week, the Silver Stirrups winner will have been decided," Lisa said.

"Hey, you're right," said Stevie.

"I wonder whether it'll be Carole or Andrea," Lisa mused.

Stevie stopped. "Excuse me?"

"I said, 'I wonder—' "

"I heard what you said," Stevie interrupted. "I just didn't like it. In the first place, Briarwood is a huge show. Junior riders come from all over. Half of them are capable of beating Carole *and* Andrea on any given day. In the second place, *you* and *I* are capable of beating Carole and Andrea. And don't you forget it, Lisa."

Lisa grinned. "You know, I had forgotten. Thanks, Stevie."

Briefly, the girls discussed the classes they were entering. Lisa thought Prancer was ready for the three-foot hunter division, but she was going to stick to two-foot-six just to be safe. And despite her success at the schooling show, Stevie was going to enter Belle only in junior jumper classes—to be safe and, more importantly, to have fun.

"Okay, so I'll see you tomorrow," Lisa said.

Stevie didn't respond. She was staring over her shoulder. Lisa turned and followed her gaze. Mr. Barry was coming out of the ice cream parlor. At first Lisa was glad to see that he had changed out of his TD's uniform. He was probably on his way home. But then she looked closer. The Tastee Delight outfit had been replaced with a second uniform. With a sinking feeling, Lisa recognized the rust and yellow of the local fast-food Mexican restaurant.

"Country Doctor's oats," she murmured, averting her gaze.

"And Andrea's entry fees," Stevie added quietly.

9

CAROLE GOT TO the stables very late Monday afternoon. Her plan was to avoid Lisa and Stevie as much as possible. She didn't want anything to break her concentration in this crucial last week. She especially didn't want discussions about Andrea Barry to distract her. Briarwood was Carole's big chance to prove that she was better. It was that simple. Lisa and Stevie couldn't understand her singleness of purpose. To them, riding was a pastime; to Carole it was much more.

As Carole groomed Starlight, she kept up a running monologue. "You're not afraid of any old fancy junior hunter from New England, are you, boy? So what if he cost thousands of dollars? You could beat him in your sleep, couldn't you?"

"Looking forward to the show?" said a cheery voice behind her.

Carole spun around. It was Mrs. Reg, Max's mother—the second-to-last person Carole wanted to see. The older woman was known for her rambling stories. Right now Carole didn't have the patience to listen to one of them. "Hi, Mrs. Reg. Uh, yeah, I guess so," she said.

She hoped her tone of voice would convey her lack of interest in talking. To her relief, Mrs. Reg moved on down the aisle. "As long as you learn something and have fun . . . ," Carole heard her murmur. "That's what I always say."

"Great, now she's started talking to herself," Carole muttered.

When Starlight was ready, she led him from the cross-ties to the indoor ring. There was one other horse working in the ring. Carole recognized Kismet. Red was riding him. He waved when he saw her.

Maybe something had changed, thought Carole. Maybe Mrs. Murphy was going to let Red ride Kismet at Briarwood after all. Carole mounted and rode over to say hello.

"Hey, Carole!" Red called.

"Hey, Red! Doing some practicing?" she asked.

Red cocked his head. "I guess you could call it that," he said. "At least, I'm making Kismet practice. He's got a big day Saturday."

Carole felt terrible. So Red was only schooling Kismet for Mrs. Murphy.

"Say, are you feeling better?" Red asked.

"Huh?" said Carole. Did Red know she'd been upset about Andrea?

"Max told me you had had a pretty bad stomachache."

"Oh, right," Carole said. She was ashamed of the lie. Her father always told her that the problem with lying wasn't the initial lie, but all the other lies you had to tell because of it. "I do feel better," she said reluctantly.

"Good, because Max was worried about you."

"Really?" Carole said, trying not to sound too interested.

Red nodded. "Yeah. He was worried Andrea wouldn't have anyone to train with this week."

"Oh," said Carole. "I see." She felt as if she'd been slapped. Red couldn't have made it any clearer. Andrea was Max's top priority. Carole had been reduced to the status of a helper! She was like a stablemate—a—a *workhorse!* She was supposed to train with the champion, challenge her a little, all the while knowing that she wouldn't be able to keep up!

Carole reined Starlight away from Kismet. "I've got to get going," she told Red abruptly.

"I'll tell Max you're up and at 'em!" Red called after her.

"Fine!" Carole said. To herself she added bitterly, "Tell him the workhorse is all warmed up and ready to go."

DESPITE CAROLE'S BAD HUMOR, Starlight was in fine form. He was fit and responsive. Carole forced herself to shake off her doubts, fears, and anger and to concentrate on the job at hand. First, she walked on a loose rein to let Starlight stretch. While he stretched, she did several minutes of limbering exercises herself. She took her feet out of the stirrups and rotated her toes. She leaned forward and touched the headstall of the bridle, then leaned back and touched Starlight's croup. She rolled her shoulders several times. Now they were both relaxed.

The next part of the warm-up consisted of trotting, both rising and sitting. Sitting to the trot was never easy. The two-beat gait could be jarring. Carole worked on keeping her back straight, her seat deep, and her elbows close to her sides, not flopping all over.

At the canter, Starlight had more to work on. Cantering was the gait next to galloping. Starlight was a half-Thoroughbred, a horse bred for racing. Occasionally, Starlight tried to keep speeding up at the canter until he *was* galloping. Carole had to make sure that didn't happen.

After twenty-five minutes, Carole was done with the flat part of her warm-up. Riding "on the flat" simply meant not jumping. No responsible rider would ever take her horse out and start jumping right away. That was how horses got injured and riders fell off.

Carole now shortened her stirrups two holes to make it easier to get up into jumping, or "two-point," position. She picked up a trot and headed Starlight toward the cross rail in the middle of the ring. Max usually left at least one cross rail up for the riders to school over. It was a good jump to start with because the X shape had a natural low point in the middle; horses automatically knew where to take the jump. Starlight was no exception. He pricked up his ears, jumped neatly, landed cantering, and let Carole slow him back to a trot on the other side. Carole took the cross rail a few more times straight on. Then she switched her approach, coming in at more difficult angles, similar to the ones they might meet in a horse show course.

Carole had now been working forty minutes. She might have continued, but she decided not to. She didn't want to tire Starlight out by jumping too much the week before the show. Nor was she having any major problems that she needed to work on. And finally, she thought, loosening her reins again, if there was one thing she knew about horses, it was that it was always better to quit while you were ahead. If she kept schooling with no real purpose in mind, Starlight would think up some major problems fast enough!

Carole had been so preoccupied by her thinking—worrying—about Andrea and Briarwood that she hadn't enjoyed riding lately. This afternoon had reminded her what it felt like to ride for the sake of riding. As she cooled out her horse, Mrs. Reg's words came floating into her head: *"As long as you learn something and have fun."* Then Carole remembered what Max had said—what Max *always* said: *"Challenge yourself and your horse."* Even her father had reminded her that she could always learn something—even from a bad ride. Although she wasn't going to admit it to anyone else, Carole realized something. It wasn't exactly a new thought, but it came back and hit her full force: The way she was looking at Briarwood, Carole doubted she was going to have fun, learn anything, or challenge herself. Fixating on one competitor prevented all those things from happening.

To be perfectly honest with herself, Carole thought, she was actually dreading Briarwood. It wasn't that she was worried about messing up—at least, not that worried. She knew what had gone wrong at the schooling show—how she'd warmed up too quickly, lost her concentration, then lost her nerve. But her newfound determination to win would definitely help her concentrate. And yet, what was the point? The whole day was going to be a grueling, ultracompetitive, exhausting fight to the finish. The horsewoman in Carole recoiled from that scenario. In her heart of hearts, she knew that the purpose of riding was what Mrs. Reg had said. If she won at Briarwood, what would it prove? Would Max go back to thinking she was his best student? Or would she have to keep beating Andrea, at every show, every Pony Club event, every everything? Would she have to try to "beat" her in lessons, too? Besides, even if she did win the trophy, it wouldn't change the fact that Andrea was a year younger. If Andrea won it next year, did that make her just as good, in retrospect? And what if, in the worst case, Andrea did beat her? How could she look Max and Stevie and Lisa in the eye?

Carole's head began to ache at the questions buzzing in her mind. She took her feet out of the stirrups and hopped off.

"Well, boy," she said to Starlight, her voice grim, "we're in it now, and there's nothing we can do except try to win that trophy."

As she led Starlight out of the ring, Carole saw a figure slip away into the barn. She hurried through the door to see who it was—and caught a glimpse of Andrea Barry disappearing around the corner.

"Of all the nerve!" Carole muttered, her brown eyes flashing. Here she'd been trying to be mature about Andrea, and all the while Andrea had been spying on her! Why the heck was she lurking around Pine Hollow so late? Didn't she *ever* leave the stables? Was she trying to beat Carole by putting in more time than her? Carole's jealousy came flooding back. The girl had everything! Couldn't she at least let Carole ride in peace?

Half crying, half sputtering with anger, Carole marched back to the cross-ties, Starlight in tow. She was going to get to the bottom of this right now. Over the years, The Saddle Club had learned to put up with Veronica diAngelo. But Pine Hollow wasn't big enough for *two* conniving spoiled brats!

CAROLE GOT STARLIGHT untacked and put away in five minutes flat. She was going to have it out with Andrea Barry once and for all. Leaving her saddle and bridle on a hay bale, Carole went in search of the younger girl. She checked the locker room and the grain room. She looked inside the barn and outside. She even went up to the hayloft. But Andrea was nowhere to be found. "She's hiding," Carole guessed, tapping her foot angrily. Then suddenly she knew where Andrea would be. Carole spun on her heel and strode to Country Doctor's stall. The chestnut gelding stuck his nose out to say hi. Carole gave him a distracted pat, then peered in. At first she saw no one. But then she heard something. It sounded like crying. Carole listened harder. It not only sounded like crying, it *was* crying, unmistakably.

"Andrea?" Carole said uncertainly. The wind seemed to have been let out of her sails.

After a minute, a small voice said, "I'm okay. Really."

"Are you sure?" Carole asked. She'd been so ready to yell at Andrea that she didn't know what to say.

"Yes, positive. Go away. I've just got allergies. I'm fine, really."

Carole remained standing outside the stall, unconvinced. A moment later, she heard Andrea start to cry again. That decided her. Gently she pulled back the bolt and entered the stall. "Easy, boy," she said to Doc. It took a minute for her eyes to adjust to the dim light. Then she saw Andrea in the far corner of the stall. Her brown hair was tangled, and her face was streaked with tears.

"What—What's wrong?" Carole asked. In spite of herself, she felt sorry for Andrea.

Andrea tried to speak but choked on her words. Finally she said, "I guess I'm just nervous about the show."

113

"You? Nervous?" Carole said without thinking. This was not the conversation she had expected to have with the new star riding student of Pine Hollow.

Andrea sniffed. "I know it sounds silly, but I've never been to a show without my own instructor."

"But Max *will* be there," Carole reminded her.

"I know, but he'll have so many other students to attend to. What if he doesn't have time for me?" Andrea asked in a small voice. "He told me himself he's going to be so busy on the day of the show that—"

"Oh, he'll have time for you, all right," Carole said flatly.

Andrea looked up, a hurt expression in her eyes.

Instantly Carole wished she could take back her remark. "I—I didn't mean that—"

But Andrea was sobbing again. "I knew my dad shouldn't have asked Max to give me so much extra time. But he wants the best for me, and he thought if I got a lot of private attention at first, it would help Doc and me adjust . . . after the move. You probably think it's silly that I had a private lesson, don't you?"

Had Carole heard right? Had Andrea's father *requested* that Max spend more time with his daughter? "No, not silly," Carole said truthfully. She tried for a lighthearted response, hoping to cheer Andrea up: "Just expensive."

114

To Carole's dismay, Andrea only cried harder. She had stood up and was weeping into Doc's reddish brown mane. Carole had done the same with Starlight many times. Her heart went out to Andrea as she struggled to find comforting words. "Look, there's nothing wrong with expensive as long as you can afford expensive," she said encouragingly. "It's just that, well, my dad doesn't really believe in spending a lot of money on riding. Or, at least, more than he already does."

"But that's just it," Andrea sobbed. "We can't afford it. My dad works three jobs to pay for Doc! Ever since my mom died, he'll do anything to make me happy! Anything! It's no good trying to tell him that private lessons and custom boots and even a horse like—like Doc won't make up for her being gone!" Overcome with sorrow, Andrea couldn't go on.

Gravely, quietly, in a voice barely above a whisper, Carole said, "Your mother's dead?"

Andrea nodded, her cheek against Doc's neck. "She died a year ago."

Carole felt the strength ebb from her legs. She leaned against the stall door. She took a breath. Then she stood up and put an arm around Andrea's shoulder. "Andrea, my mother's dead, too," she said.

* * *

115

WHENEVER LIFE GOT too intense, The Saddle Club had one tried-and-true remedy: They went on a long trail ride. "Wait right here," Carole said to Andrea, when they had both managed to stop crying. Andrea looked confused but agreed. Carole left the younger girl and hurried to the other end of the stalls. Although Starlight and Doc had been worked already, a trail ride wouldn't have done them any harm. But Carole thought a change of horse would be good for both her and Andrea. After checking with Mrs. Reg, she ran and tacked up two of the school horses, Delilah and Barq. Then she led both of them outside to the mounting block. "Okay, Andrea!" she called.

When Andrea appeared, Carole said, "We're going trail riding. No ifs, ands, or buts about it."

Before Andrea could object, Carole handed Delilah's reins over and mounted Barq. Andrea seemed shocked into obedience. She sprang neatly onto the palomino's back and followed Carole to the head of the trail.

". . . so when I lost my mom, I threw myself into riding, too," Carole was saying twenty minutes later.

"I know," said Andrea. "I mean, I didn't know about your mother, but all I ever hear around here is how dedicated Carole Hanson is, how good Carole

Hanson is. Can I be honest? It's sort of hard for me. You see, at my old barn, Doc and I were the stars."

Carole couldn't believe her ears. "But you're the stars here, too!" she blurted out.

"Yeah, maybe for about an hour—since we did well at the schooling show. But you should hear Max go on about you. He keeps telling me I ought to ride with you because I would learn a lot. Today he said I should go watch you school Starlight so that I could figure out how to ride without an instructor at my side all the time."

"He *did!*" Carole exclaimed. Her heart felt lighter than it had in days. How could she have been so paranoid? With a rush of remorse, she remembered all the misjudgments she'd made about Max and Andrea over the weekend.

"And he told me how you trained Starlight yourself. I could never do that," Andrea said wistfully. "It's all I can do to control Doc. I've let him get into so many bad habits that he's a one-woman horse now. Nobody else can do a thing with him. Whereas Starlight has beautiful manners, doesn't he?"

"You know, I never thought of it that way. I was so embarrassed that I couldn't make Doc behave the other day," Carole said.

"And I was so embarrassed that you saw what a spoiled horse I have! I'm a little better with him now, but I've let him get his own way for so long that it's tough." Suddenly Andrea's voice had a catch in it again. She rode Delilah up beside Barq. "But even if he is spoiled, Carole, I'd die if we had to sell him! I don't know how long Dad can keep up this schedule! It's awful for him, just awful. You should see how tired he looks . . ."

Carole listened thoughtfully as Andrea described her father's three jobs. Then she put on her best teacherly voice. Andrea was in need of guidance, and Carole was going to give it to her. After all, she was one year older, and at least one year wiser. "In the first place," she said, sternly but kindly, "has it ever occurred to you that you could help keep Doc?"

Andrea frowned. "Not really, no."

"Well, you can. Stevie and Lisa and I help out at Pine Hollow almost every afternoon. We muck stalls, groom, get horses ready for lessons—whatever Max needs done. If you were willing to work, Max might be willing to make a deal with you. Maybe he'd charge less for board or give you some free lessons. And secondly, you don't need all the fancy equipment you have. You could sell some of it and make money that way. Part of being a good horseperson is being inde-

118

pendent—not needing to be babied. You're an excellent rider, Andrea. You don't need an instructor at your side every minute. You don't need the most expensive custom-made tack. You can do it on your own."

Carole glanced at Andrea to see how she was taking all this. Andrea was staring at her in amazement. "How did you get to be so independent? You're only a year older than I am!" she cried.

Carole thought hard. "I guess my father taught me that," she said. "He taught me that feeling sorry for yourself never helps."

"That sounds like good advice," said Andrea.

"Yeah," said Carole, her mind drifting back to the talk she'd had with her father after the schooling show, "except when you misinterpret it."

"Huh?" said Andrea, puzzled.

Carole smiled as she nudged Barq into a trot. "Once in a while I forget that taking responsibility for yourself doesn't mean making enemies of everyone else," she said.

The girls trotted through the woods, eventually looping back toward Pine Hollow. It was evening now, but the late spring sun had not yet set.

"So I guess this horse show stuff is old hat to you, huh?" Andrea said, as they walked the horses cool.

"Sort of," Carole admitted. "You too, right?"

"Not really," said Andrea. "At least not anymore. Doc and I have won a lot up North. But Briarwood should be a real challenge—new courses, new judges, new competition. I just wish I had my old coach here. Just to help us get our bearings . . ."

There was that word again: *challenge*. It seemed to be haunting Carole. It bothered her. It almost felt as if someone was trying to tell her something.

"Hey, you girls are out late," said a voice.

Carole turned and saw Red. He had finished raking the aisles and was taking a rare moment off to watch the horses at play in the near pasture.

"Yeah, we had some things to discuss," Carole said.

"Say, why don't you let me take Barq and Delilah in?" Red offered. "You probably want to get home to dinner. It's a school night, isn't it?"

Carole and Andrea tried to refuse, but Red insisted on helping. Finally they handed over Delilah and took Barq themselves. On their way in, they met Max, hurrying out. "You girls finally went riding together," Max observed. "Good."

"I can sure see why you said Carole's going to make a great instructor someday," Andrea said.

Max beamed. "I hope so," he said, elbowing Carole, who had turned bright red at the compliment. "But

I'm afraid she might bail out and become a veterinarian instead. Then Dr. Barker and I will have to fight over who gets to hire her."

Carole watched Max's rapidly retreating back. She couldn't believe the turn the day had taken. That was the nicest thing Max had ever said to her in her whole life. Maybe her dreams weren't so crazy after all! If Max thought she could be an instructor someday, maybe she would! She felt as if she were brimming over with happiness. And all because Andrea Barry had been crying and Carole had comforted her!

"DAD," CAROLE SAID at dinner that night. She'd gotten home so late that they were eating take-out Chinese at the kitchen table. "What do you do on base when there's a bad situation and it turns out for the best? How do you celebrate?" she asked.

She expected her father would have to think about his response for a minute. But Colonel Hanson answered right away. "Easy," he said. "You always give back to the troops."

"What do you mean?" Carole asked, twirling noodles around her chopsticks.

"If something great happens that makes my job easier, I turn right around and try to share the wealth. I try to show my appreciation by giving something to

121

the men and women who work for me. I try to make their jobs easier. Any good leader does. Does that answer your question?"

"What if the troops weren't exactly working for you?" Carole asked.

"The same principle applies, honey, whether it's your coworkers or your boss or your friends or your family. You should try to give more than you receive. It's not always possible, but sometimes it is. Any time you can afford to be generous, you should be. And speaking of generosity," Colonel Hanson said, his dark eyes twinkling, "pass the lo mein, would you?"

ANDREA PICKED UP the phone on the second ring. When Carole told her she was going to have an instructor for the show, Andrea shrieked with joy. When Carole told her who the instructor would be, she shrieked again. "But what about Starlight?" Andrea asked, concerned. "He's all trained and fit and ready to go."

"I know," said Carole. "Don't worry about him. He's not going to stay behind. I'm lending him to a friend."

Then Carole telephoned Max.

"I hope you don't think I'm copping out," she said. "Heck, I hope I'm *not* copping out. But I'm not riding at Briarwood. I decided to help Andrea instead. She thinks she needs an instructor, and I said I'd help."

Max's brief answer removed any doubts she had: "Carole," he said, "I'm proud of you."

That left just Stevie and Lisa. Would they be proud of her? Carole sighed. It was going to take so much explaining. She would have to make them understand that the decision had been hard, and yet she knew it was the right thing to do. A part of her still wanted a showdown with Andrea. A big part of her wanted the Silver Stirrups Trophy shining on her bookshelves. But she *had* a lot of trophies shining on her bookshelves. She didn't often have the chance to give something back to the people she cared about and to help someone in need. Carole sighed again. Before she got into any of that stuff, she was going to have to explain about Andrea: that she wasn't a spoiled brat, that her mother had died, that her father worked three jobs . . .

11

"GIVE ME A coffee—black," Carole said.

The man behind the snack bar filled a Styrofoam cup. "That'll be sixty cents, lady," he said. Then he saw who had ordered it. He raised his eyebrows. "You're sure you want this? Black?"

Carole nodded. All the other riding instructors drank black coffee at horse shows. Why not her?

Walking back to the Pine Hollow van, she took a sip. It was utterly disgusting. She decided she would walk around with the coffee instead of actually drinking it. At least that way she would look legitimate.

The van area was bustling with activity. Carole

paused to take in the sight. Usually she was so busy getting herself ready that she hardly had time to appreciate the scene a horse show created. But today she could. The morning rain had stopped and the sun was coming out. Horses and riders hurried to and fro, each pair looking more polished than the last. That reminded Carole that she ought to be getting her charge ready for the first class.

At the Pine Hollow van, Red was helping Stevie, Lisa, and Andrea get ready. Because Max was so busy with his adult students, Red and Carole had volunteered to take over the juniors for the morning.

"Carole, will you give me a leg up?" Lisa asked, trying to hold Prancer still. "Prancer's living up to her name this morning."

Carole gave Lisa ten fingers to help her mount. "Good luck, Lisa. Now, don't let her get lazy," she advised.

"Lazy? But the fences are only two-foot-six. We're used to jumping much higher at home," Lisa said, straightening her hard hat with one hand.

Carole swiped Lisa's boots with the rag she was keeping in her back pocket. "Exactly: She might be bored with the jumps today. It's up to you to keep her awake."

125

As soon as Red went off to warm Lisa up, Carole found Andrea. She was getting dressed in the cab of the van. "Come on, Andrea, you should be getting on soon," Carole told her.

"I know, but I'm just so nervous," Andrea said. "My dad's here, you know. He took the day off so he could watch me. And everybody looks so good. I—"

"Enough. You've got to banish all those thoughts. You'll feel much, much better once you're on. So hop to it. I'll get Doc out of the van."

Carole had to hide a grin as she turned away. She couldn't believe how much she sounded like a real instructor!

Carole unloaded Doc, who had been bathed, braided, and saddled. Like most experienced show horses, he didn't seem at all fazed by the commotion. That was good. If he stayed quiet, Andrea would relax, too. "I'm counting on you, boy," Carole told the chestnut. Doc cocked an ear forward. "I'll take that as a promise to be good," she murmured.

Soon Andrea had mounted. Carole carried Andrea's coat to the warm-up area and put Andrea right to work. There was no point in standing around. It only made the horses tired and the riders nervous. Carole joined the instructors who were barking out commands in the middle of the grassy circle.

"Heels *down* over the fence, Linda! How many times do I have to remind you?"

"Don't let him pull, Robby! Get his head up!"

"Three-two-one—now! Nope. Too late. Circle around and do it again!"

Carole took a deep breath. "Looking good, Andrea! Looking really good!" she yelled.

An older woman with a leathery face and a cigarette hanging out of her mouth addressed Carole. "That your sister?"

"No, she's my student, actually," Carole said, hoping she sounded natural.

The woman took a drag on her cigarette, her eyes momentarily on Andrea and Doc. "She's good. Nice horse, too. My kid's on the bay." The woman pointed to a smart-looking horse. "Hey! Hey, Paula! Yes, I'm talking to you! What'd I tell you about your outside rein? Shorten it up! Right up!" the woman yelled. Then she turned back to Carole. "These kids—you tell 'em twenty times, they get to a show and forget they ever took a lesson. What can you do?"

Carole had to stifle a grin. "Just tell 'em again, I guess," she said. "All right, Andrea! Trot the cross rail! Heads up over the cross rail!" she belted out.

"Hey, we gotta get over to the ring, but good luck today," said Carole's new friend.

127

"You too," Carole said, trying to sound nonchalant. But she had only one thought: *I talked to another instructor!* She couldn't wait to tell Stevie and Lisa.

THE NEXT COUPLE of hours went by in a blur. Andrea responded perfectly to Carole's coaching. All she really needed was someone to confirm that she knew what she was doing. Once Carole figured that out, she had her instructor's role down pat. In the first class, children's hunter over fences, Andrea and Doc practically floated over the course. Andrea came out of the ring ecstatic.

"Wasn't he great, Carole?"

"The best. And you weren't bad yourself."

"I hope we get something," said Andrea.

"Don't worry about that now," said Carole. "Keep him walking. The flat class is sooner than you think."

"Who is that girl?" Carole heard a woman at the rail say. "I wonder where she rides."

"That's Andrea Barry on Country Doctor," Carole said. "She's a student at Pine Hollow."

The woman nodded.

"Oh, Pine Hollow," another woman said. "Of course. Max Regnery runs a tight ship. He always does well with the juniors."

"Oh, yes, that's where that Hanson girl rides. She's

really made a name for herself in the local Pony Club."

Carole gulped. It was all she could do not to shout aloud. *That Hanson girl? A name for herself?* Grinning wildly, she went to join Andrea. Before she got there, though, the results were announced over the loudspeaker. Andrea had won. Paula Grossman, the girl on the bay, was second. Carole hugged herself with joy. The morning had started off beautifully.

STEVIE AND LISA sat listlessly in the front seat of the van. The morning had gone all wrong. "I can't believe Prancer and I had two knockdowns!" Lisa said. "In the two-foot-six division!"

"That's better than Belle and I," Stevie countered. "A refusal and a run-out! And now we're not in either of the jump-offs! The show's over for us before it's even begun!"

"It's so embarrassing!"

"You're telling me!"

"Prancer was lazier than she's ever been!"

"Belle was totally out of control!"

The two girls were silent for a moment, munching on the french fries they had bought to cheer themselves up. Neither of them could understand what, exactly, had gone wrong in their morning classes. The more depressing thing was that neither of them had entered any afternoon classes.

"Why the long faces?" said Carole, poking her head through the window. She had come back to the van during the lunch break.

"Don't ask," Stevie and Lisa said at the same time.

"Oh. Bad morning?"

They nodded.

"We just don't get it. We were so prepared!" Lisa said.

"We only entered things we knew we'd do well in," Stevie chimed in.

"Ah," Carole said. "I get it."

Stevie and Lisa were surprised. "What do you mean, you get it?" said Stevie.

"Oh, come on," Carole replied. "You can't tell me this hasn't happened to you before." At her friends' blank looks, Carole continued, "You were overconfident, that's all. You thought it would be easy to do well."

Stevie and Lisa looked at one another. "So, you mean we didn't try as hard as we normally would?" Lisa said in a small voice.

Carole nodded.

"Hmmm . . . ," said Stevie.

"Gee . . . ," said Lisa.

"It makes sense if you think about it." Carole hesitated, wondering if she should continue. She didn't want her friends to think she'd become Miss Know-It-All, just because she was serving as Andrea's instructor for the day. But she *had* come to a realization. "You know how Max always tells us to challenge ourselves?" she said finally.

Stevie and Lisa nodded, warily.

"It's not because he wants us to do badly. It's because he wants us to do well. He knows we'll do better if we ride at the highest level we're capable of riding."

Stevie and Lisa had to agree that it did make sense, when Carole put it that way. They'd never ridden so conservatively—or so badly—in their lives, at least not in competition.

"But don't look so glum," said Carole brightly. "You can still make something of the day."

"How?" said Stevie. "From what we've heard over the loudspeaker, you've got Andrea's coaching pretty much under control."

"*Very* much under control, I'd say," Lisa agreed. "Two firsts, a second, and a third? She must be thrilled."

"She is—but she's nervous, too. She's tied for children's hunter champion right now. It's going to come down to the last class, children's hunter hack. And the

131

same person who beat her in equitation is tied with her in the hunter division. Everyone's betting one of the two of them will get the Silver Stirrups," Carole explained.

"Everyone?" Lisa asked. "Like who?"

"Oh, I don't know specifically. That's just the word among the instructors," Carole said coolly. "Listen, Andrea has me for the afternoon. But there's somebody else who has no one to help him, and it's his first show."

"Red!" Stevie and Lisa exclaimed. They didn't need to be asked twice. They sprang out of the van and headed for the rings.

"He's warming up outside of ring number three!" Carole called after them.

"Okay!"

"Say hi to Starlight!" she yelled. She figured a simple hello didn't make her an overprotective owner.

12

"WHY DID I ever agree to do this?" Red asked.

Stevie and Lisa smiled. Red O'Malley—cool, calm, collected Red O'Malley—had a classic case of nerves. Both girls knew what that was like. The jumps looked bigger than before. The competition looked tougher. And, invariably, they would ask themselves why they had ever decided/agreed/volunteered/asked/hoped/prayed to compete in the first place. They would also swear that they would never go to another horse show as long as they lived.

There were only two more riders before Red. The girls watched him run a shaky hand down Starlight's neck. Clearly, a pep talk was required. Together they gave him one. Stevie told him he was an excellent rider, that he was better than most of the competition. Lisa told him he was riding a talented horse. An experienced horse.

"Think positive," said Lisa.

"It's only twelve jumps," said Stevie.

"Prepare, prepare, prepare," said Lisa.

"It will be over before you know it," said Stevie.

Finally they sent Red off with a swipe of his boots and a pat on Starlight's rump.

"We're rooting for you!" they both called.

"IT'S ALL MENTAL," Carole was saying. "You've got to think positive. You know you're better than the competition."

"But what about that girl Paula, on the bay?" Andrea said.

It was understandable that Andrea was anxious, Carole knew. Doc and the bay were tied for first, and Paula had just ridden a near-perfect course. Carole was about to launch into a list of things the other girl had done wrong, to prove to Andrea that she was beatable.

Then Carole remembered the problem with that strategy. "Forget about her," she said. She put a hand on Doc's reins and looked seriously up at Andrea. "The worst thing you can do is fixate on one rider like that. It ruins your concentration. Believe me—I should know," she added.

"When did you ever do that?" Andrea asked. "I'll bet you're just saying it to make me feel better."

Carole shook her head ruefully. "I wish I were," she said. "I wish I were."

"The jumps look huge," Andrea said a moment later.

"Just remember to take your own advice," Carole told her student. "Prepare, prepare, prepare."

"Okay," Andrea said, tightening her girth one last hole.

Carole sent Doc off with a pat on his chestnut rump. "Hey!"

Andrea stood in her stirrups and turned around. "Yeah?"

"I'm rooting for you!" Carole called.

"BUT MAX, I JUST don't see how poor little Kismet is going to jump those huge fences," Mrs. Murphy wailed.

"Kismet is sixteen-point-three hands high," Max said patiently. "Believe me, he can do it. And you can do it, too. You've just got to think confidently, keep yourself organized, and—"

"I know, Max, I know: Prepare! But sometimes I

forget to prepare, and then we get into trouble, and— Oh, gosh, I almost forgot. My husband's watching. There he is! Bob! Bob! Look, he's waving! Max, give him a little wave, will you?"

Sighing deeply, Max turned and waved at Mr. Murphy, who was sitting in the spectator stands of ring two. *Where the heck is Red?* Max wondered. Surely the juniors were almost finished? Had Red fallen asleep in the van? Max frowned. That wasn't exactly great behavior for the head stable hand of Pine Hollow.

"Oh, Max, I'm so nervous!"

Max refocused his attention on his student. He gave the brown gelding an encouraging pat. "Don't be. Just do your best, Mrs. Murphy. You're capable of beating anyone here."

Max watched the older woman gather up her reins and go off to jump. He rubbed his eyes and took a sip of black coffee. It had been a long day of instructing. He'd gotten up at five, and he'd been on his feet all day. Even after the last class there would be a lot to deal with. There were horses to be rubbed down, legs to be wrapped. There were bran mashes to be made, a van and two trailers to be cleaned out. There were congratulations to be given to the winners and consolation to the losers. Plus there were the regular evening chores to be done. Once in a while, at times like this, Max wondered why he ever allowed/encouraged/ required his students to ride in horse shows at all. Then he saw Mrs. Murphy pick up a canter and clear the first fence with inches to spare. Max smiled. Suddenly it was all worth it.

MRS. MURPHY RODE well, for her, but she didn't win a ribbon. So Max was mildly surprised when, walking back to the van, he was accosted by another instructor. "Hey, nice job today!" the woman called. "You guys really cleaned up!"

"Thank you," Max said uncertainly. He continued walking.

"Hats off to Pine Hollow!" a man in a tweed coat cried.

"Big day for you, huh, Max?" said one of the judges.

"Briarwood's been kind to Pine Hollow, eh?" called Jock Sawyer from aboard his jumper.

Max stopped in confusion. Had he missed something? Then, out of the corner of his eye, he saw three of his students running toward him. It was Stevie Lake, Lisa Atwood, and Carole Hanson—*The Saddle Club*, Max thought wryly.

"Yay, Max!" Stevie cried.

"We did it!" said Lisa.

Carole grinned shyly.

"Did the three of you win blue ribbons that I'm not aware of?" Max asked in puzzlement. "No, that can't be right. You're not even riding, Carole. Okay, what gives? Why are my colleagues congratulating me?"

"Well, you see, Max," Stevie began, stalling for time. So many times, Max had an exciting announcement for them, but he would hold off making it to build up the suspense. So now Stevie relished the chance to withhold information from him. But Lisa and Carole, oblivious to her plan, began pouring out the news.

"So then Red—"

"So then Andrea—"

They didn't get far. They didn't have to. Right then, Red O'Malley and Andrea Barry came trotting up on Starlight and Doc. There was a red second-place ribbon streaming from Starlight's bridle. Andrea and Doc had two ribbons: another first, and the red, blue, and yellow championship ribbon for winning the children's hunter division. They all watched Max to see how he would react. He smiled. Then he grinned. Then he threw his head back and laughed aloud.

"I have one thing to say and one thing only," he said. "I *love* going to horse shows with you guys!"

* * *

BACK AT THE VAN, everybody pitched in to help rub down the horses and get them ready to ship home. Lisa took out the horses' braids. Stevie went around with a bottle of liniment, cotton, and bandages, rubbing forelegs and wrapping them for shipping. Carole groomed and buckled on light blankets, or "sheets." While Max and Red cleaned up around the van area, Red filled his boss in on his decision to ride in the show. "Once Carole said I could take Starlight, I couldn't wait to compete. A horse like that . . ."

Carole, glowing with pride, threw her arms around Starlight's neck.

Even Mr. and Mrs. Murphy appeared. They had apples and carrots for the horses and cookies for the riders. Mrs. Reg took all the ribbons won by Pine Hollow students and strung them up in the cab of the van. Finally, every horse and every rider was ready to go. Except for Andrea and Doc. Andrea was still dressed in her riding clothes. Doc was still tacked up. Seeing them standing alone, waiting, Carole's heart went out to Andrea. This was the most excruciating part of a show—even worse than getting nervous before jumping. Andrea knew she'd done well enough to be up for the Silver Stirrups Trophy. She knew the judges were making their decision right then. If she won, she would ride over to the ring and collect her trophy. If she lost, she would have stayed tacked up and ready for nothing. Her father was up in the stands, also waiting. Carole had been in the same position many times. She went over to try to distract Andrea.

"Hey, what's a trophy, anyway?" she joked. "A big hunk of silver that you have to keep polished, right?"

Andrea smiled. "Thanks, Carole," she said softly. "You're a great instructor."

Carole tried to brush off the praise.

"No, I mean it. You understand because you've been there," Andrea said. "I never could have done it without you."

Embarrassed, Carole looked away. To think she'd wanted to ride Andrea into the ground a couple of days ago! To her right, Carole saw another horse and rider pair, tacked up and waiting. It was the girl, Paula, on her bay. Beside the pony was the instructor. Carole waved, and the woman waved back.

"Whatever happens, great job, you guys!" the woman called.

"You too!" Carole called.

She and Andrea heard it at the same time: the crackle of the loudspeaker as the PA system came to life. Carole crossed her fingers. She saw Andrea swallow hard. After a horse show, Carole knew, you could remind yourself that winning wasn't the point, that you had learned a lot and had fun. But right before the judges announced their choice for the best junior rider of the day, it was pretty darn hard to remember.

And, of course, they always droned on and on. "We'd also like to thank our chief judge, Mrs. Hayes, the local foxhunt, the Pony Clubs . . ."

Carole crossed and uncrossed her fingers. Was crossing two hands bad luck? She couldn't remember. Her palms were sweating. It was as if she herself were up for the trophy. Doc jiggled his bit. Andrea swallowed again.

". . . and finally, we would like to announce the winner of the Silver Stirrups Trophy. As you may know, this is the first year this award has been given. The silver cup was donated by Mrs. Eugene Lyman of Meadowland Farms, in honor of . . ."

"Gosh, will they *ever* get to the point!" Stevie wailed behind them. Her comment did it—it broke the tension. The whole Pine Hollow crowd began to laugh, even Andrea and Carole. They laughed until tears were streaming down their faces. They laughed so hard they almost missed the point, when it came.

". . . Barry, of Pine Hollow Stables."

The loudspeaker was temporarily drowned out by cheering. Her reins loose, her stirrups barely on her feet, Andrea set off at a trot, grinning madly.

"Come on, you guys!" Stevie called.

". . . newcomer to the area, on her chestnut Country Doctor, winner of three firsts . . ."

Carole looked to her right. The other girl had dismounted. She was fighting back tears. Her instructor put an arm around her shoulders. Over the girl's head, the woman gave Carole the thumbs-up sign.

"Better luck next time!" Carole mouthed. Then she set off at top speed after the rest of the Pine Hollow contingent. There was celebrating to be done—Silver Stirrups style!

13

BACK AT PINE HOLLOW, the horses were in bed in no time. After giving Starlight his umpteenth hug of the evening, Carole looked around for Andrea, to say good-bye. She thought she might find her in the tack room, but Mrs. Reg was alone, hanging up a few last pieces of equipment.

"I think Andrea left already, dear," said Mrs. Reg. "She and her father had a lot to talk about."

Carole nodded. She understood. After the show, Mr. Barry had had a long talk with Max about keeping Country Doctor at Pine Hollow.

"Do you think they'll work something out?" Carole

143

asked anxiously. After today, she realized, she would be truly upset if Andrea had to leave.

"Oh, yes," Mrs. Reg replied. "She's too good to quit now."

At Mrs. Reg's comment, Carole felt a twinge of jealousy. She looked up at the Silver Stirrup Trophy. Andrea had left it on the windowsill so that everybody at Pine Hollow could share it. In a way, Carole wished it were hers, all hers. She certainly wasn't done with competing. But she also knew that today she had learned more than she ever would have had she battled it out with Andrea. There would be time for her to ride against Andrea in the future. Maybe she would win, and maybe she wouldn't. Either way, it wouldn't affect how she felt about herself. Thinking of herself as the best junior rider at Pine Hollow had been pointless anyway, not to mention vain. If she should strive for anything, Carole realized, she should strive to become the most accomplished horseperson she could be. Instructing for a day had certainly helped her toward that goal.

"So, Carole, you're the big winner today, hmm?" said Mrs. Reg.

Carole looked up, not sure she'd heard right. "What do you mean?" she asked.

"Both of your students performed extremely

well—Andrea and Starlight," said Mrs. Reg. "I'd say that makes you a winner twice over."

Carole flushed at the praise. She smoothed her fingers over the ribbon in her pocket. Red had given it to her and insisted she keep it. It was funny, Carole thought: A week ago, a second place had seemed like the end of the world. Today it seemed like a wonderful beginning.

"I guess Briarwood is cursed for me!" Lisa declared. She and Stevie burst into the tack room, laughing and talking. "Last year I took Prancer before we were ready. This year we were *too* ready! I just can't win."

"Well, then it's blessed for Carole," Stevie said. "Last year she met Cam, and this year she made her debut as a top instructor." Cam was a boy whom Carole had dated, off and on, until he moved away.

Carole missed him, but right now she didn't feel like thinking about anything at all sad. "Hey, did I mention that I even tried to drink black coffee?" she asked.

"And did you swear?" Lisa asked.

"And chain-smoke cigarettes?" Stevie prompted.

Mrs. Reg looked appalled. "My Max doesn't do any of that," she said in a shocked voice.

"Oh yes I do, Mother," said Max, joining them.

"Max!"

Max grinned. "I drink black coffee," he said.

"How do you do it, Max?" Carole asked. "I thought it was disgusting!"

Max leaned toward her confidentially. "Trade secret. I guess that means you'd better stick to riding for a while, Carole, despite your early success as an instructor."

"Enough of this chitchat," said Mrs. Reg. "I've got spaghetti and meatballs on the stove. Max, your wife is making garlic bread, and Red just went to buy a case of soda. We have enough food to feed an army. You girls are invited for dinner."

Stevie whooped louder than if she'd just won a blue ribbon. Carole and Lisa were more reserved but incredibly pleased all the same. It was a rare, rare treat for the Regnerys to invite them to stay for dinner, and they'd get to see Maxine, Deborah and Max's new baby.

Putting their arms around one another, The Saddle Club followed Mrs. Reg and Max out of the tack room. On the way in, Stevie started to make up a song, and Lisa tried to stop her. Stevie had a terrible voice, but now that she had something to sing about, nothing was going to stop her. Carole just laughed. It was a perfect ending to a perfect day. She hoped that someday Andrea Barry would be as lucky as she was.

ABOUT THE AUTHOR

BONNIE BRYANT is the author of many books for young readers, including novelizations of movie hits such as *Teenage Mutant Ninja Turtles* and *Honey, I Blew Up the Kid*, written under her married name, B. B. Hiller.

Ms. Bryant began writing The Saddle Club in 1986. Although she had done some riding before that, she intensified her studies then and found herself learning right along with her characters Stevie, Carole, and Lisa. She claims that they are all much better riders than she is.

Ms. Bryant was born and raised in New York City. She still lives there, in Greenwich Village, with her two sons.

What were The Saddle Club girls like before they rode horses? Find out in Bonnie Bryant's next exciting Saddle Club adventure . . .

BEFORE THEY RODE HORSES
Saddle Club Super #5

Max's wife, Deborah, is about to have her baby, and The Saddle Club girls are keeping her company before she goes to the hospital. Stevie, Carole, and Lisa all recall—in their own words—what their lives were like before they rode horses, and how they've never been the same since.

Stevie: Having three brothers meant I was always a tomboy, but it also meant that my older brother and my twin brother were better than me at just about everything we did together—soccer, touch football, even Kick the Can! It might sound selfish, but I wanted to be the best in my family at something—at *any*thing!

Lisa: To say my mother is class-conscious is putting it mildly! She's always had lots of ideas about what a "young lady" should be good at doing. But does an eight-year-old really need *charm school*? I think a "young lady" should be good at something because she loves doing it. I wish someone had told my mother that.

Carole: With my dad in the Marines, we moved around a whole lot when I was little. It really got lonely, always being the new kid in school, trying to make friends with complete strangers, and then having to move when I finally did make some friends. Do you know what that's like?

Saddle Up For Fun!
Join The Saddle Club

As an official Saddle Club member you'll get:

- *Saddle Club newsletter*
- *Saddle Club membership card*
- *Saddle Club bookmark*
- *and exciting updates on everything that's happening with your favorite series.*

Bantam Doubleday Dell Books for Young Readers
Saddle Club Membership Box BK
1540 Broadway
New York, NY 10036

SKYLARK

Bantam Doubleday Dell
Books for Young Readers

Name _____

Address _____

City _____ State _____ Zip _____

Date of birth _____

BFYR - 8/93